THE
SUNFLOWER
PROTOCOL

Andre Soares

A Novel

This is a love letter to all black women. The ones who raised me, the ones who fed me, the ones who loved me and allowed me to lead. The ones who suffered harmful stereotypes, profiling, abuse, and endured the pervasive grip of systemic oppression, fighting a thousand battles on multiple fronts.

This is the most genuine expression of my love for you.

As you inspired my works and shaped my trajectory, I was blessed with the opportunity of exploring the beautiful complexity of your characters, of what makes you, first and foremost, simply... human.

The Sunflower Protocol is the outcome of years dedicated to the craft of storytelling; a sculpture of clay reshaped over countless cycles. I truly hope you enjoy it.

Special thanks to my cover designer, Francisca Mandiola, and my editor, Ashley Olivier, instrumental figures without whom none of this would have been possible. I treasure your consistency and your faith in my vision over these past few years.

CONTENTS

CHAPTER 1
SKELETONS ON THE COAST

15th Revolution

6th Moon

At the edge of time. You. Always.

The body washed ashore, sinking into coal-black sands, denying an aggrieved rip current.

Upon his forehead, a fresh gunshot wound pelted with salt imposed a crater-shaped mark, one oozing darker shades of reds competing with the surrounding pink waters. His eyes opened to an epiphany.

The man was alive, a rogue speck of sand on the Namibian coast, an anomaly among the shifting dunes inevitably pouring into the ocean. A small caliber round exited his forehead, rejected like undesirable foreign matter; the compressed casing splashed the incoming waves and vanished with them.

There was pain in his glacial, steely eyes, yet hope displayed through a liberating smile.

He was a sane madman, a survivor of the treacherous columns of time and space.

But his pale porcelain complexion made him a target in this new world. He was the snake in the garden of Eden, the vector of conveyance for forbidden knowledge.

Soon, a drone boomed in the skies, shaking the dry sands the man painfully crawled to. Shots erupted beyond the dune, foreshadowing another equally painful examination of ballistics.

Someone, or something, was coming for him. *Amahle, please.*

On the brink of exhaustion and severely dehydrated, the survivor fainted, crashing against the hot black sands his hands dug into.

The stranger jolted awake, snatched from a dreamless place by the rumble of an engine.

They were coming. He could barely see, his vision still blurred by a sharp pain that seemed to split his skull in half. However, he could still hear the machines converging towards him, menacing and rabid.

Three, maybe four. He turned on his back, trying to ease his discomfort by soaking in the blazing sun.

Closer. The engines roared, like territorial animals sensing a potential dispute. Soon, they shut off. A commanding voice shouted, "Am... the pale devil. There. Yeh!"

Voices began to rise. Something fine had slipped through his fingers, a reminder he could still *feel.*

Sand. The pink skies above guided the last brush strokes of a strange, otherworldly spectacle.

The voices gained speed. And proximity.

"Assess, Yeh."

Someone held him in place and locked his jaw with a strong grip. Delicate floral scents starkly contrasted with the roughness of the skin. *An elegant killer*, the man thought.

"Who are you, demon?" she demanded, but her voice held a softness.

The survivor tried to speak, but he was mute. Tears welled up in his eyes. The outline of a second face approached him. *Amahle?*

"His eyes. The waters have taken them. I need the *Isi*."

He could not move, left at the mercy of giants whose ruthless determination and delicate tones confused him.

Someone spread his eyelids wide, forceful. Another set of hands dropped a sizzling liquid into his damaged optics.

From the short-lived pain soon emerged a divine revelation: the faces of goddesses. The man smiled, tears of joy cuing the end of a state of shock.

He sat, fingers still digging into the soil. Perspectives leveled. The black sands, the pink waves, the red skies... There were six elements, dark-skinned women whose understated elegance screamed royalty. And among them, his love.

He breathed, "Amahle?"

One of the queens stepped forth. Her ballerina frame and tight bun complimented a sepia undertone. He recognized her grace, her reserve; this quiet, underemphasized strength akin to natural leaders.

He remembered the first instances, the glances, the goodbye hugs that quickly turned into morning embraces. She was his and he was hers, and those were the only labels they subscribed to.

However, something had changed. In her stance, in the very windows of her soul.

Here, on this foreign land, she was a weapon, and her beautiful brown eyes did not reciprocate his love.

She towered over him, armed to the teeth, and asked, "How do you know my name?"

"How? You mean the world to me, Ama." The nickname triggered protests among the crowd. "Your name is engraved *within*, beyond time and space."

They locked eyes. She was hostile to the contact, further pressing her fingers against his sharp jaw. In more favorable circumstances, he would have found that play more appealing. Yet here, it was rage and indifference that drove her questioning.

"We've never seen pale flesh like yours in this world. I do not know you."

"My name is Rome."

"This does not tell me anything." She made him stand with remarkable ease. "Who are you? You speak our language."

"I am your husband." The skies borrowed from darker hues. "Something sent me here. I needed to try. I was hoping—"

Amahle slammed the survivor to the ground, applying massive pressure on his frame. She picked him back up. The others remained still, emotionless mannequins from her exhibit.

"I asked for the truth, demon."

He looked at her, and the joy that had at first inhabited him vacated his soul, deconstructed in the vacuum of her other self. Or maybe her new self.

Rome objected, "I'm no demon. This is the truth."

Amahle looked behind and nodded at another goddess. This one was even more soulless, purposely belligerent in her defiant stance.

Amahle stated, "Yeh. This is a code one."

The one called Yeh simply answered, "Yes, Administrator."

Rome saw the one he claimed was his significant other quickly shift her weight forward, striking his airways. He fell and started suffocating, his tensed neck unable to relieve an invisible pressure applied to his trachea.

Amahle raised her rifle and squeezed the trigger. Shots penetrated his flesh, strategically positioned to shut his vital organs down.

Rome's eyes rolled back. Then, came the darkness.

The killers stood by his corpse, heads down, and mouthed undecipherable words in a litany against fear.

The waves rid his crooked frame of the blood oozing through his open bullet wounds.

His pale flesh almost burst as the bullets shot back out. Amahle and her unit took a few steps back, scanning the nearby dunes and edgeless waters.

The group readied and riddled Rome with a new salve of perforating shells.

After what felt like a never-ending massacre, the rifles were silenced. The smoke dissipated. An ochre smell lingered, mitigated by the ocean breeze. Rome's flesh was disfigured, bloated with instruments of death.

Another wave washed ashore.

The outer layers of the survivor's skin were frantically twitching, fighting to eject the foreign matters that poisoned his body. Amahle raised a hand to avert another shooting, her eyes narrowing on the scene before her.

Rome regained consciousness multiple times, drifting in and out of collapsing episodes.

Another wave crashed.

Amahle stepped forward. She found hope in his eye flutter, as she bridged the gap between them, uncertain.

She crouched and ran her fingers through the scarred tissues of his freshly healed wounds.

BOOM.

The contact propelled her out of stillness, to a dreamworld of fewer boundaries, in a sequence of impact sounds.

The survivor, Rome, was there too.

CHAPTER 2
A MAZE OF LIFE

"What have you done?!" Amahle shouted at Rome, distancing herself from the stranger, leaning on the high wall of a colorful corridor. Her voice echoed in the boundless space.

"Nothing, Amahle. *This* isn't my work. It's not." Rome's jaw clenched. "But I sense memories in this place, I can't quite explain it, but it's here."

"Memories?" she pressed.

"Of us."

Amahle's eyes danced on the enclosures of this maze. They were covered in flowers, majestic in their colorful blooming and strong aroma profiles. The floor was hardwood, an odd pattern of swelling circles.

Her Namibian kingdom and its advisor, Iwalewa, had conditioned her body and soul for potential clashes of titans, beasts of prey sweeping her cities and deserts, forbidden magic flooding the lively streets of her stronghold. This man, however, was a unique threat: something more relatable, more personal, smaller in scale yet deadlier in blow.

By design, Amahle was taught to hate the white devils hiding beyond the *Void*, cowards sheltering in lands they could not reach. But she had always been cautious with the folktales of her world, a fractured place operating through a warped lens.

After all, where was the tangible evidence? Until today, no pale flesh like Rome had ever made contact. Was he truly evil? *Possibly. Most likely.*

Rome pulled her out of her contemplation. "Amahle, I understand this may defy the natural order of things. And I don't have all the answers yet. But I knew this one thing, when I crashed your shores, propelled to your world by something I can't name. I belong here. I was sent to find you. Again."

Amahle was on the verge of tearing up, her heart pressed by a force she could not quantify. But the foreigner's dreamworld projection had treated her with such gentleness despite the murderous rampage she indulged in, out in the real world.

Something was driving him, a sentiment that echoed beyond the revengeful noise the enemies of her kingdom often displayed. An emotion so pure she could not label.

Strangely, she realized she felt safer in his presence. He offered a hand. She refused.

They began their journey, walking deeper into the maze.

His tall stature cast a shadow on the unexplainably bright floral compositions that enriched their path. Amahle trailed cautiously behind, prepared to slay the suave monster whose outline flickered in the dimmed lighting.

Amahle looked up, but there was no light source, only darkness; yet, somehow, a light shone.

They reached a corner. To her, the smell was familiar, homey. Orange wax and a summer breeze.

There's a disconnect, Amahle thought. *Why is this smell comforting? It is not from my world.*

Ahead, within the confines of a second corner, stood Rome. He had walked to two barrel chairs flanked by accent tables, objects of a cluster in the otherwise empty space. She stopped as he ran his fingers through the chairs' fabric, slightly pressing on its rounded edges.

"This was our peace. Our silent bonding. Just you and I, shielded from mad and loud things." Rome's tone was neutral, devoid of inflexions, neither forceful nor preachy. He did not try to sway her or argue a point, and she simply followed.

In this place, she was no longer a ruthless prophet; she was getting acquainted with a part of her that never realized before *him* happened.

Rome broke the silence as he stood still, contemplating the setup. "There was this quiet understanding. The tall structures. I cannot name them. The heights. But everything felt so grounded. So right. There was no need to argue the silence. We simply existed within that world."

He continued, "Can you feel it, Ama?"

Amahle was in tears, fighting to straighten her posture and dry her eyes. Rome resumed his advance.

"Dad! Not fair! Ahahahah!" said a small silhouette running in the maze ahead. Her footsteps were muted as if she raced on clouds.

The little human turned around and faced Rome; Amahle peeking over his shoulders. The little girl's Bantu knots shone on her sun-kissed complexion.

Beyond the next corner, past the child, a voice echoed, unseen. Amahle's.

"Imani! Dad and I too strong! Here I come; you can't hide!"

The little girl turned again and continued down the labyrinth, laughing a joyful noise.

Rome let out a few tears. Amahle stopped. She yelled, "Demonic!"

The man motioned *no* in a nod. "This is no parlor trick, Ama. This is fate. A tangible fate. Our Imani. I remember her now." He paused. "Did you feel deceived, or hopeful? Or maybe even confused?"

Amahle tried to process the sight of a daughter who borrowed features from her and Rome, in almost every aspect. The small, sharp nose, the high cheek bones, the green-hazel eyes, the brown skin and darker hair... What did she feel? At this very moment, Rome's question felt painfully relevant.

They continued.

Soon, the flower maze opened to a larger space with floor tarpaulins and drapes made for a patchwork of off-whites and creams. It was stained with paints. Easel stands with massive canvases filled up the space, illuminated by a gorgeous natural light whose provenance remained a mystery. The two dreamers stopped at the sight of their clones, the latter oblivious to their presence.

Rome-2 and *Amahle-2* were sipping and painting, drawing grotesque African masks. There was the same proximity *Rome-1* mentioned when they entered the maze.

The *-2s* radiated in love, in an effortless display of something that felt so... right. The broad strokes they began to apply to a shared canvas shaped a bloated face whose carved eyes were unintentionally dreamy.

Rome-2 asked *Amahle-2*, "That's how you feel?"

The two burst into laughter, initiating a paint fight where bullets came in teals, mauves, burgundies, and golds. The lighthearted exchange brought a warm smile to *Rome-1*'s lips. *Amahle-1* was still confused, even more so furious at her ignorance of the facts, at her discovery of a world that should not exist.

The clones disappeared, evaporating with the remainder of the scene. There was nothing left but bare sand. Coal-black sand.

Reality had set back in. Amahle and Rome had collapsed on a Namibian beach, struck by tremors, their eyes rolling back in a macabre fashion. Yehudith and the rest of the unit had taken a few steps back, waiting for the seizures to fade.

Soon, the bodies slowed down, twitching at irregular intervals. Amahle's distant gaze told a thousand potential stories. She was now curled up in a fetal position, rocking back and forth. Rome frantically dug the sand, thrashing around in pain.

Yehudith ordered, "Enough. Bring the Administrator to *Gogo*! I'll take the demon to a cell."

Another wave crashed, more permissive and less aggressive, almost... compliant.

The unit left the scene with their leader, disappearing behind the high dunes.

With them also journeyed Rome, the prisoner who had evaded time's reach.

CHAPTER 3
IWALEWA

The spacious jail cell was well-lit and fully furnished, a relatively comfortable holding area contradicting the violent narrative pushed by his handlers. Neutral tones of a delicate smelling linen upholstered a bed and a corner chair, complimenting a white desk with a glossy finish and a lavatory hidden behind a smoked plexiglass separation.

Rome knew he was in a captive state, however. The derogatory language, the rough transport, the absence of communication or representation all summed up one simple fact: He was a caged monster, the *white devil* who spat rifle shells back out.

Rome did not know why he had been shielded from physical death, but it was a minor concern to him at this very moment, as he navigated through the capricious currents of his repressed feelings.

In the confines of his fragmented mind, Rome knew Amahle was his savior, not his captor. He welcomed death and pain, as his wounds healed fast, tightening the flesh of his battered body.

Sitting on a detention mattress, Rome gazed beyond the

front-facing glass wall, grateful to have survived a journey without her.

I love you, Ama.

Amahle was rushed to a state-of-the art medical facility, her eyes fixed on modern ceilings whose patterns ran intersecting lines.

Around, questions flooded as she underwent a brain CT scan, voices lost across an insulating veil. The tight space she fitted in to endure testing was oppressive, preventing her from processing what had just happened. She silenced the fears.

Medical personnel gravitated around the droning machine, collecting data.

"Toxicology reports came back clean."

"Hematology reports indicate normal levels. No fluctuations in white blood cell count."

"So, there's nothing apparent?"

The doctors and nurses went silent, unable to produce a viable answer, leaving room for a humming, buzzing backdrop that fed off of confusion and tension.

Among such professionals, one individual had refused to partake in the ongoing conversations. The elderly woman, with her quiet demeanor and unassuming frame, did not belong to the medical corps or the militarized unit that brought Amahle back to the city.

Inside the machine, a skeleton of ring lights, Amahle was moving again; she was pulled out on a conveyor, welcoming the sterile operating room lights with relief.

The elderly woman approached her, while the others flocked to her scan imaging.

Amahle tilted her head sideways and smiled at the lady.

She said, "Iwalewa."

Iwalewa answered, "How are you, child of the sun?"

"Confused, *Gogo*."

"The man?"

Amahle nodded in agreement.

Iwalewa smiled and laid a comforting hand on her forehead.

She tutted, "Ama, they will find nothing in that brain of yours. Your experience was less... grounded in reality. Or maybe it was, but not in *ours*."

"I saw another life, a child. But he never tried to sell me on the idea, he merely *showed* me. What is happening *Gogo*?"

Iwalewa looked at her prodigal child, an inflexible yet fair leader she saw blossom over the years. She answered, "Amahle. I think Time with a capital T has caught up with us. Our ancestors gave us an opportunity to solve the biggest mystery there is. *Òkùnkùn. Inkungu.* The Void."

Around, some of the medical corps' side conversations suddenly died, faces frozen in restraint.

Amahle swept the personnel with her eyes, seeking further reactions. She asked, "Hm. *Gogo*, will you question the stranger for me? I want to avoid prolonged contact for now."

Iwalewa nodded in agreement and said, "Yes. '*Lezimphuphu zemibala ngezabahambi abafana nawe*'. I will use the pigments, the ones for the travelers. You rest, Ama."

Amahle waved the last advice away and sat.

Her eyes found the doctors, nurses and radiologists congregating around printouts of her CT scan.

Amahle asked, "Diagnosis?"

The staff turned towards her, faces relaxed and holding benevolent smiles. A younger woman whose delicate figure stood out replied, "No brain nor nerve damage, Administrator."

Rome stared at his reflection, the vision of a breathing corpse inflating and deflating on the vitreous pane of his jail cell.

He had won, no matter the outcome. Although he had no recollection of his journey, he knew, somehow, that leaping from timeline to timeline, from faraway worlds to faraway worlds, was the best gift he could have been granted.

There were no names, dates, or locations stored in his temporal lobe besides Amahle's and Imani's. Nevertheless, Rome already knew of certain truths, told by a muted voice inhabiting his shell, a busy sensory input that was felt rather than heard or seen.

Who was he to question the grander scheme of things? His soulmate, the one he was certain he had traveled for, found him; no amount of segregationist framework, torture, slander, and psychological warfare could take that away from him.

The thick ballistic glass of his holding cell opened. A couple of Amahle's warriors and an older figure walked inside his cage in a dignified silence. They showcased self-control, confidence, and situational awareness.

Rome braced for another attempt on his life, anticipating the thousand painful resurrections that would follow.

"I need to talk to Amahle," he said, sitting on the plush layer of his mattress.

The three refused to respond. They probed the man's flesh with neutral eyes. His heart beat loud against the walls of his jail.

Finally, the two warriors left. The elderly woman raised a hand, casting a shadow on Rome's pale features. *Less physical, yet still commanding*, he thought.

She reminded him of a divine intervention: inevitable, undisputable, inescapably transformative.

She spoke. "Rome? My name is Iwalewa. I am here to understand. We share this objective, hm?" She lowered her hand. "You will not see Amahle until she consents to such. *If* she ever does. Consent is common knowledge here. Is it *there* too?"

Rome had entered new uncharted territories: diplomacy. Iwalewa was... unusual.

She resumed, "I don't believe in torture, Rome. And even though our oral history associates your kind with evil spirits, I never really subscribed to this... mode of inheritance. That makes us both pariahs."

Iwalewa sat beside Rome, calm and unassuming.

For a few seconds, she stared into an infinite pool of existential thoughts, and continued, "But my people's safety remains a priority. So, Rome, I need you to set your own expectations aside for a moment and explain yourself. Can you?"

Rome looked straight ahead, afraid to find comfort in her benevolence, afraid she could weaken his resolve or compromise his vision. He nodded in agreement, however.

Although she was older, Iwalewa exuded beauty. Her Havana twists brought volume to her hawk-like sharpness. She looked up and exhaled, revealing the simple elegance of her being. "Good. So, tell me, why are you here? And how do you cheat death?"

The survivor relaxed his shoulders and took a deep breath, embracing the tightness of his closed wounds. The cell was clean and orderly, odorless, structured. Meanwhile, his mind was chaotic, fractured, and scattered.

He said simply, "I don't remember the world I come from, nor how I made it here. I have language and motor skills. I'm self-aware. I have imageless visions. I remember smells, sounds, textures... It's all mixed up. And painful, like I am a piece of a stretched patchwork. I don't know about the bullets… I… All I know is that I was sent to accomplish something of significance with Amahle, the love of my life."

Iwalewa smiled. "She doesn't know you, Rome. You are like *ubungozi bomuntu ongaziwa*. Stranger danger."

The saying opened his face to a familiar meaning. He objected, "I love her. Always will. Beyond anything else. I think she saw—"

Iwalewa interjected, eyes narrowed, "After she made physical contact with you?"

"Yes. We shared this lucid dream. We had a child. A daughter. Her laugh was contagious. And the smells, the profiles… It was home. Amahle knows it."

Iwalewa scanned the cell for a few seconds. It was… humane. The hallways were quiet; very few of her people ended up here.

She ran her spiderlike fingers across her face, from top to bottom.

"Rome, these visions. Your purpose… You understand we can't just take a leap of faith and act on those? We need assurances, concrete proof. And this is why I'm here."

The glass doors in front of them closed. Rome attempted to stand but was pinned down by pressing fingers he never foresaw.

Iwalewa retrieved a half facepiece chemical mask from her pocket and applied it to her honed visage. Columns of smoke flooded the room. Rome was kept still by her supernatural strength while the gas agent robbed him of his motion. He was soon paralyzed, sitting on his detention mattress like a bent mannequin.

The cell's ventilation turned on and quickly extracted the smoke from the room. Iwalewa removed her mask and retrieved a small cube made of a colorful, friable material of various shades and undertones from her vest.

In Rome's peripheral vision, the shape of her broke the cube into a fine powder resting in her right palm.

She paused and looked up once more.

"Rome, regulate your breathing."

His chest protested the paralysis, furious in its mad patterns of contractions and expansions.

"You will not die. You *cannot* die. This is the best solution we can offer. This temporary paralysis you were… afflicted with will prevent fall injuries, as we determine the veracity of your claims. Again, breathe."

Rome understood, and although he had full confidence in his given purpose, he still feared death, even now that he was presumed immortal. But what lingered in his damaged thoughts was the possibility of losing Amahle again, the destruction of their bond as she drifted away from him, out of fear or anger.

Was she influenced by what seemed to have been decades of misguided xenophobia among her people? He hoped she followed the path Iwalewa claimed to have taken.

He began regulating his breathing, attempting to accept that he was no longer loved by all, or most, but instead challenged.

Iwalewa observed the man. She found beauty in his love for Amahle. In this world, most connections were established for political purposes or financial benefits. Ironically, she thought, Rome brought colors to this palette, this monochromatic composition.

The ideas he brought will survive this containment. She raised and faced him.

The powder from the friable cube was spread on his face, sticking and sizzling upon contact with his skin. The pain was beyond anything known to mankind, but his lips were sealed. The powder liquefied and entered his pores.

Iwalewa held his face, looking into the windows of his soul, glacial eyes of a cold charm. The visions began dancing on his ocular globes.

There was Amahle, sitting at a café with Rome, in a city roamed by many people. Too many. Giant structures stretched the neighboring perspectives, exacerbating the angles of a pedestrian street. They were laughing, comfortable in each other's presence.

The other eye showed Amahle bearing a child, walking alongside Rome on a beach that bore striking differences with Namibia's *Skeleton Coast*. Iwalewa saw nothing but love, compassion, and devotion.

God's powder, as they called it here, had spoken its truth. Rome's truth.

It was real. In another timeline, in another world, he was hers, and she was his.

Iwalewa released her hold.

She said, "You are truthful. There is a possibility she sees that too. But you need to be patient. You need to let her process things. And you need to understand that Amahle is her own—"

Suddenly, the ground shook. An invisible shockwave rocked the space, pulsing at regular intervals. Around, time came to a halt, then resumed its course. Sirens rang afar. Staggered steps resonated in the hallway as Iwalewa held onto Rome.

The two warriors who had left earlier ran to her rescue, but she waved them away. She ordered, "Someone! Stay with him. Keep him safe!"

As the waves grew feebler, dialing down, Iwalewa disappeared, her shadow flying on the walls.

CHAPTER 4
IS THE DEVIL OF PALE FLESH?

Time kept on expanding and retracting. It was an odd feeling, a race to the edge of a cliff; one repeatedly stopped in its track, then resumed before breaking off once more.

It was the buzzing of bees, the screams, the water streams, and silence. Time was navigated through in bits, challenging volatile short-term memories.

Rome felt dizzy as he regained his full range of motion, scrapping off a dried coat of mud from his face. He had no intention of escaping, instead enduring the shockwaves passing through the walls like the ghosts of a darker past. Nonetheless, he was concerned for Amahle's wellbeing.

He asked his handler, "Is Ama safe?"

"This is no—"

Silence. A pitch-black cage where even the most intrusive thoughts had no voice.

Time resumed.

Rome inquired again, "Is she?"

The stern woman of razor-sharp bone structures ignored his

request, holding him still while pointing a rifle at the glass doors. Rome remembered those weapons. They brought death.

She moved them forth and peered in the hallway; it seemed to duplicate and extend to infinite patterns.

"What have you done, demon?!"

Rome objected in a louder protest, "This is no—"

A void. All things gone in a vacuum. The very fabric of reality erased. Full containment.

Time resumed.

Soon, the wrecking force retreated, and the stretched visions ceased. Time stabilized to again fit in general relativity.

The guard grabbed Rome's undone collar and shoved him forward. "You follow my lead, clear?"

He responded with an absent stare, "Clear."

They engaged the hallway whose staggered cells apertures showed no prisoners.

Some of the cells were painted in pink, some in an off-white tone, like Rome's. Noticeably, they all possessed a different layout. At the end, a sharp turn led the two to a planetarium with a holographic sky vault; their footsteps clicked on the concrete flooring, giving the replicated stars above a certain depth of field, a magnitude.

Rome's handler was speeding, rushing at a non-sustainable pace. The prisoner pushed through, however, anxious to confirm Amahle was still breathing, living up to the untold stories of her resilient nature.

Another wide hallway led to a giant terrarium enclosed in a massive glasshouse whose cylindric shape shot upward to stratospheric heights. Rome, seeing through a shaky lens, thought, *This is more than a detention center.*

The guard slowed their course as they followed a natural-looking trail shaped in tortuous curves.

"No tricks, white man, clear?" the handler snapped as she came to a halt.

Rome agreed in silence.

Before them extended a wider antechamber, and a gigantic door.

A synthetic voice subjected the guard to questioning, its neutral and monotone speech reaching from speakers mounted in the ceiling. "Refer to your HPR. Please be advised that the challenge question is a one-time use resource. Tier 1 Sec."

The guard answered, "Process."

The virtual intelligence resumed, "Who can whistle from another man's mouth?"

"The other man. Six Nine Three C."

The steel door slid open. A bright light shone, inviting. Rome's escort kept pushing forward, relentless in her momentum, sweeping left and right with her death-bringer.

As they stepped into the open world, screams of terror added *vision* to Rome's blind sight. Black specks filled his eyes as he attempted to make sense of what had just appeared before him, bathed in light.

Death. Bodies with no apparent trauma, and fires with no apparent source. Lush gardens and pathways consumed by time loops, their withered greens fading to darker undertones.

Small, squared structures whose walls crumbled were left precipitately, the doors and windowpanes cracked open. Lost children were swooped in by some of the very same women Rome had encountered on the *Skeleton Coast*.

So much beauty in this place. Did I cause this?

Rome's thoughts wandered to hypothetical grounds. His handler drove him left to a downslope, towards the beach. Soon, they veered right to an underground access, and another chamber sealed behind a vault-like entryway. The word *DECON* was painted on the ground in red lettering, drawing Rome's interest.

The guard pulled the heavy door open and proceeded inside; the chamber's boundary automatically closed behind them. She pushed Rome forward and shouted, "Stay still."

She placed her personal effects and weapons on a conveyor belt to her right and posted behind the prisoner.

Above, an automatic fire suppression system triggered and showered Rome with a mist-like solution. He startled, leaning against the left wall as if possessed by fear-inducing hallucinations.

"DON'T MOVE."

Rome's eyes sought his handler as he returned to his spot. The next decontamination agent was dry, waterless, and odorless. The process was sequential, three gradually longer steps employing a set of color-coded compounds: white, red, black.

The automated system shut down quietly.

"Move forward. Three steps," the guard ordered.

Rome obliged, facing another steel door. He was shaking, acclimating to the recent fluctuations in temperatures expected of this procedure.

The chamber repeated the process for the handler. Soon, the mist dissipated.

She shouted, "Yeh, e be much."

A voice replied from an intercom placed right of the door frame before them, "E be tings, Iso."

It unlocked and opened wide. Rome was pushed forth down a ramp.

Behind him, the decontamination room disappeared,

surrendering to artificial lights flanking their sides. They reached and entered a room whose walls were marked with the word *PROCESSING* in white lettering.

Across from a bolted stainless-steel table stood Amahle and Iwalewa. A few elements from her praetorian guard formed two rows on the right, covering a nearby access.

Rome breathed a sigh of relief. She was alive.

Nonetheless, Amahle seemed antsy, moving her thumbs around her knuckles in a circular manner.

She suddenly bridged the gap between them and applied pressure on Rome's windpipe, her grip tightening around his bruised throat.

He struggled against her hold. "Enough, Ama!"

She pushed him against the closest wall, pressing the barrel of a handgun on his forehead. The scarred tissue from his previous wound caved in under the strain.

"Enough, Ama."

Amahle inched closer, menacing. "You crashed my world, cheated death, and now brought plagues."

Iwalewa approached and laid a hand on Amahle's shoulders. "Ama, he was truthful."

Amahle took a few steps back and looked at one of her soldiers, the elegant killer Rome met on the coal-black sands.

The soldier said, "They just had another wave."

Amahle nodded and asked Rome, "Why are you here?"

Rome defied her accusing tone and replied, "I was... brought here with a few memories of you. I can't quite explain it, but I can *feel* things. It's like my life trajectory colliding with yours, for the greater good."

"For what purpose? Speak," Amahle demanded.

"I don't know. Everything is... it's tied to you, somehow. What does this world need, Ama?"

She sneered. "Do not call me Ama."

"You used to love this nickname. In moments where you felt lost, you used to ask me 'What does this world need?'."

Amahle stole a brief glance at Iwalewa. "*Òkùnkùn*, Rome. The Void."

Rome inquired, "What is it?"

Her looks could kill, anger consuming her features. "At the edges of this world, my world, there are barriers. Leading to a place where time and space have no boundaries. A place no one has ever returned from."

Rome tried to process the information. He had washed ashore.

"Is it where I traveled from?"

"You washed ashore, and since the Void neighbors the deep sea too, it's likely. You survived it, somehow."

Rome massaged his forehead, fighting a splitting headache. He resumed, "Is this... Void growing?"

"No, but it restricts us. One day, all of our resources..."

A silence settled. Rome's accuser, Amahle's second-in-command, tensed.

He tried to piece it together, visualizing a dark fog of war blending in with the horizon. "Maybe we should explore this."

The rest of the group objected in a language Rome could not comprehend yet whose tone was unequivocal. The elegant killer was looking at her watch, counting a pattern in the cacophony of protests, unbothered and quiet.

She told Amahle, "No more loops. I think we should go."

Silence settled once more.

Amahle approached Rome. Her eyes narrowed like a lioness on the prowl. "We'll keep you under close watch until further notice. One wrong move and I'll find a way to bring death to your doorstep."

The two were separated, with Rome exiting the bunker first under close guard. He looked over his shoulder, stealing one last glance at the woman he had lost yet still loved.

CHAPTER 5
I AM MY SISTER'S KEEPER

Dead people, Ama.

The voices of her internalized thoughts tried to rationalize what laid before her eyes.

Corpses, stiff and discolored. Burnt corneas trapped under white ice crystals. Faces frozen in discomfort, as death struck unforeseen. No hemorrhaging, no signs of blunt trauma.

Amahle was walking amidst the mass casualty event, now turned into a triage area, stealing a glance at her second-in-command's watch through polycarbonate lenses hooked onto an oxygen circuit.

Beep.

No shockwave. No time loops.

Against the backdrop of a constant hissing, Amahle's voice asked, "Yeh. I need the med corps to be thorough. We need to establish patterns on what caused their death. There are common symptoms prevalent here. Early onset of rigor mortis, skin discoloration, corneal disease... Surveillance timestamps show this area was exposed to harsher time loops. Longer breaks, faster accelerations."

Yehudith acknowledged her words with a nod, silent in her response.

The two were labeling bodies and personal effects, shaded by the swinging leaves of giant trees, treading carefully in their protective equipment.

Around them, glass structures had withstood the cataclysmic event. The marketplace was quiet, drained of its boiling blood, its war chest taxed in the aftermath of an unexplainable *time storm*.

Amahle came to a halt after tagging the last casualty and studied a concrete pathway to her left, one woven into a patchwork of colorful flowers that had survived the plague. Further down the trail, the ocean glittered in pink shades.

"Administrator!" A young woman in a hazmat containment suit rushed to Amahle, holding a tablet-like device with hands whose fingers drummed on its edges.

"Yes?" asked Amahle.

"Dalimi, ID 01120702. General forensics. Some results came through."

"Please, Dalimi."

The forensics expert tilted her head in agreement and consulted her handheld device.

"No contaminated land indicators. That includes ground water migration and human exposure. There were no viruses, bacteria, or toxins employed. Toxicology reports came clean on the spectrum. Most of the casualties suffered cardiac arrest and aneurysms. We are still investigating. But you will find that the common denominator is the coverage. All fatal casualties were found within a mile radius of this specific area. Beyond this established boundary, populations survived, despite experiencing mild symptoms such as disorientation and dizziness."

Amahle and Yehudith swept the area, looking for a contributing factor through the lens of sharp eyes and various conscientious beliefs. There was no unusual element, no catalyst. Amahle crouched and laid a gentle gloved hand on the curly grass.

It absorbed the slight pressure, pleasantly spongy in its response.

"An epicenter. Dalimi, what about the structures?" Amahle pointed at the glass buildings, modern in their cubic lines and sharp angles.

"Yes, Administrator." Dalimi struck a few keys on her virtual keyboard. "Interestingly, glass structures maintained their integrity. Concrete, clay, and wood sustained heavy damage. There were no associated casualties in either instance, however."

Amahle looked up and ran her fingers across the surface of her helmet, from top to bottom. Yehudith and Dalimi followed suit, in a sequence.

A brief silence ensued.

Amahle resumed, "Okay. We need a feasibility study. Yeh, please contact the engineer corps. I want every building converted and families relocated within seventy-two thousand wave periods. Good job, Dalimi. Anything else?"

Dalimi stared at Amahle, mesmerized by her commanding stature. For decades, oral history had conveyed countless tales of the Administrator's accomplishments; how the Hive, a collective she founded, defeated the *Eye* up north, the *Inkunzis* to the east, and unified the world under the banner of a peaceful, cosmopolitan society.

"No, Administrator. It's an honor."

The Administrator's dark lenses were fixed onto the forensics expert. "The feeling is mutual, Dalimi."

Dalimi nodded, bowed, and left the scene.

Amahle and Yehudith took their helmet off, embracing the cool breeze brought from the ocean front laying further out. Yehudith departed without a word.

Soon, Amahle was alone, standing in the middle of an exhumed mass grave.

Her mind reeled. Was the plight of citizens living in a newfound fear *his* doing? Deep down inside, another idea had grown more powerful, more contagious: Was Rome the apocalyptic messenger, rather than the root cause?

Time is near.

She thought of the casualties, dozens of individuals presumed safe under the shield of her justice and the spear of her might; productive contributors of a society who favored advancements and breakthroughs. Necessary cogs in this well-oiled machinery.

One that was derailed.

Her time had come, she felt. The uncharted territories she conquered, the tribes she federated, the basic laws of fundamental human rights she brought to people whose ancestors died by the blade for a belief... It was all bound to collapse, cracking under the growing pressure exerted by new dangers.

The advent of an extinction, she thought.

Her mind fired at will, exploring the hypotheticals.

Would this foreign feeling Rome mentioned, love... would it have changed my perspective? Brought tears I never shed?

Amahle stepped out of the quarantined zone. Her feet led her to the trail she had studied earlier.

She was now headed towards a glass structure by the beach,

one that appeared to be carved by the crashing waves of the pink sea.

The sheet of glass faced west, bowing down to a majestic sunset exposure. This was no prime real estate, no center of leisure, however; it was a place where the kingdom exercised its sovereignty. It was the hotbed of a hard response, a breeding ground for Namibia's utilitarian ideas.

Amahle stood inside the very same structure, an odd architectural exercise whose slanted walls suggested there was only one acceptable stance: forward-leaning. Her praetorian guard, the Hive, sat around a massive conference table set up with notebooks, pens, and dried fruits. Amahle's collective had sworn to a hard life cultivated in frugal habits. They had brought this belief system to the fanciest milieus, adding to the mythos of the most-feared military force in *her* world.

She found her balance among the pummeling waves she stared at; she remembered the wars, the blood rivers, the shell casings sinking in the wet dirt. *The Last Unification* was an ugly segment of her history, but after what the elders called the *Great Fracture*, and the emergence of the Void, her world was thrown into political and social unrest. Now, she had to act.

When she reached her tenth year, holed up in obscure sewers, suppressed by a textbook case of ethnic cleansing against her people, Amahle formed a group of like-minded girls who were raised by their terrifying life circumstances. *They* became the Hive, the most feared authority known to this world, and its most loved.

The leader turned around and approached the table. She remained standing.

"Yeh."

Yehudith was sitting across from her, docile, compliant.

She replied, "We started conversion. Nothing conclusive on the quarantined zone yet. People are inside, but how long can we hide? You and I both know this is no life for them."

Amahle asked, "And those time storms, that's a local event, oh?"

"Yes."

Protests erupted among the Hive members.

"You cannot leave your people, Ama!"

"We have to take the *white devil* with us and march."

"No! Throw him in there, where he belongs. *Òkùnkùn* will rule."

"We have to be measured. We represent the people."

Amahle raised a hand. Silence poured.

"This." Her sisters turned to her. She resumed, "This is a sisterhood. *Ubudlelwane bodade*. An iron guard that crushed the evil *Eye*. An advocate for a more grounded society, orderly policymaking, unification. But right now, you are no better than the one you despise, oh! Maybe you are doing the white man's work?"

Amahle half believed her last words, but she had to appeal to her sisters' notion of self-awareness. She had grown closer to Iwalewa, an advisor of mysterious origins who always preached more moderate views, and Rome had brought a new perspective after he crashed into her life. He claimed love, fiercely and proudly, even under distress, as he was stretched thinner. She started considering the idea that maybe... maybe their skin color was less relevant than currently believed to be.

The visions of this dreamworld shared with Rome supported a theory she had long debated with her *Gogo*: Certain beliefs and behaviors were not tied to a specific tribe or physical features but rather to a particular upbringing, a distinctive social environment.

Amahle continued, "If we venture into uncharted territories, into *Òkùnkùn*, we may never come back, leaving our people to face an uncertain future without proper governance. But time itself is this monster, this beast who hibernated for too long. And now, it is coming for us. How long until we crumble from inaction? It's complicated. The bond that unifies us is strong, and our calling unwavering, no matter oh. So, what do we do? What would *Gogo* say?"

Yehudith raised her hand. Amahle nodded.

"We go, Administrator. We kill *it*. We take the white demon with us."

A loud silence settled.

Yehudith resumed, methodical and measured in her speech, "We kill the *Dreamwalker*, sister."

CHAPTER 6

INTO THE VOID I PLUNGE

A glasshouse. The guards don't venture outside the building. The landscaping is lush, concealing. The quietness. This is a remote location? A less restrictive containment, too. Less of a prison, more of a guest house. Hm. I ought to ask.

The guard roaming the massive room of light accents was inflexible, cold, and calculated.

Maybe not... now.

A set of bypass doors opened to Rome's left. He grabbed one last scoop of rice and cleaned his hands, leaving the plate before him empty.

Amahle entered and raised a hand. The roaming guard bowed and left.

Rome found himself facing the woman he had always loved and admired, in many lives, in countless worlds. Her curls were shining with a healthy bounce.

This... scent of hers triggered a chain reaction within Rome's shrieking mind frame: a lightweight oil, volume, a hazelnut-like aroma. *Argan oil.*

She was certainly beautiful by society's standards, he knew, but there was more to her. Amahle was this radiating soul that improved everything it touched, someone whose beauty was not intimidating but rather evocative of a joyful picture.

Rome smiled. Regardless of the outcome, he was proud and grateful to have been hers, in this faraway land he no longer remembered.

Amahle remained neutral to his loving gaze. She sat across from him and stated plainly, "I still don't trust you."

Rome kept quiet.

"But I made a decision. Do you have questions before we start?"

Rome ran a finger across his forehead. "Yes, Amahle. What happened out there?"

Amahle pivoted on her chair and looked straight through the giant glass pane behind her, staring at the mighty jungle whose greens swayed under a delicate breeze. She turned back around.

"There was an incident. A 'time storm', for a lack of better terms. Time stopped and resumed its course, repeatedly, at regular intervals. This is what you experienced in your cell."

Rome asked, his disjointed mind filled with painful recollections of the apocalyptic visions that had accompanied his transfer, "Any casualties? I played no part in that."

Her face conveyed skepticism. "We'll determine whether you have or not. I'm not at liberty to discuss losses with a stranger."

"But I'm no stranger. And deep down, you know that."

Amahle kept her expression stoic. She raised a hand and ordered, "You will follow me now. We'll review operational details and evaluate your fitness."

Rome wondered, *For what purpose?*

However, he knew Amahle had a lot to process, and unlike him, she had a home to upkeep, a society to run, with all of its complex variables and intersecting vectors.

He decided to comply without objecting.

The two stood and exited the room through the same bypass doors Amahle utilized. Ahead, two steel doors were mounted on an elevator shaft. Amahle touched the metallic coating to the right of the frame, and the elevator access opened. The two engaged.

Ding. They began their descent.

Amahle added, "This time storm had an impact on certain structures. Concrete, compressed earth, clay... Glass seemed to endure the stress better. None of that applies to the underground. The event only affected surface-level items. We believe it is directly tied to the molecular structure of certain materials."

Rome first struggled to grasp the relevance of this comment. But quickly, he remembered: Amahle mentioned an operation. *This could be useful information.*

He said, "I understand. But I'm not a soldier. I'm a messenger, maybe a survivor. How do I fit in that?"

"Can you die?" Amahle asked.

Rome's face widened in disbelief. "I'm not sure I'm following, Amahle."

"You can cheat death, so certainly you can find the courage to fight. There are fewer consequences."

Rome debated the reasoning internally. There were still consequences, damaging fears left lingering in his tissue with every death. But he was here to follow a higher purpose and reunite with the one he loved.

And she's a soldier here. Maybe a war is unavoidable.

He answered as the elevator stopped, "For you, I would."

Amahle stared at him for a few seconds, her face betraying nothing of what went on in her impenetrable mind. They engaged a hallway giving to a massive room.

X's were taped on the floor in a grid-like pattern. Fitness equipment and weapons complimented various other machines, some of which Rome could not clearly identify.

There was no one on this floor. No team, no medical personnel.

"Yes, it's just us," Amahle said, confirming his observation. She began powering monitoring equipment, massive digital displays whose big white numbers fluctuated in an erratic pattern. Amahle continued, "You'll get basic training for what's to come. The other option is detention."

Rome looked at Amahle, amused. Her threat was credible, but her presence alleviated the fears.

He asked, "What is to come?"

Amahle paused. She stared at the numbers, fleeting data running through her intense brown eyes.

"As you know now, our world is bordered by the *Void*, a dark depression no one ever returned from, a place where time has no boundaries, no laws. Millions of wave periods ago, we found scrolls buried in the sands, on the *Skeleton Coast*, where you appeared. They spoke of legends. The 'Great Fracture' is one of them. The stories also claim that someone, or something, had caused this depression and that the perpetrator was still inside."

His brows furrowed. "Still in there?"

"Yes. The *Dreamwalker*. The master of time. There were mentions of evil spirits inhabiting the lands beyond the Void, also. Your kind."

Rome objected, "All I carry is love."

Amahle ignored the comment. "Once our people are safely housed, we will depart and enter the Void from inland. Then, we will kill the Dreamwalker."

A silence blanketed the space as Rome processed the implications of this suicide mission. He was virtually invincible, but she was not. Although her strength forced admiration, he understood there was only one viable angle in this madness: to protect her with his life.

"In some of the northern cities, they say 'we no dey here to chop life'. Let's get to work, Rome."

This was one of the first mentions of his name in a way that did not suggest his imminent beheading. Something, even minor, had shifted within her. He nodded in agreement.

Amahle pointed at weapons placed on a table. The two approached.

She picked up a rifle and presented it to Rome. "This is an assault rifle. It kills. Like a castrated bull." She ran her finger over an aperture on the cylindric barrel. "This is the ejection port."

Amahle pulled a foregrip back; it slid through a cut made on the barrel, a precise incision running down to the chamber. The ejection port revealed an empty tube.

"You will make sure this is clear, unless you are ready to fire."

She handed the rifle to Rome, watching his grip, looking for something in his glacial eyes. He slid the foregrip back and checked the ejection port. "Clear."

Amahle grabbed a magazine set up nearby. It was loaded with bullets of various colors showing through the clear material.

"This is your magazine," she instructed next. "You will slam it inside this opening on the bottom of your main grip. The bullets will then be loaded in the rifle as you slide the foregrip back. There is no safety, so be careful."

"What are those colors for?" Rome carefully accepted the magazine and examined its contents.

"Red, incendiary bullets. Green, extra penetration factor for armored targets. Black, higher velocity for range and accuracy.

Brown, poison. This last one is used to send a message. More political."

Rome slammed the magazine in.

Amahle raised a hand. "Before you load it, always exercise muzzle awareness. Always point it down range." She pointed at targets beyond the table. "Never at a fellow soldier. *Never.*"

Her last word carried weight.

"Understood, Amahle." Rome slid the foregrip back. A metallic sound echoed through the vast space. He found a free spot by the table and looked at her.

She said, "Ready? Aim at this target. Before you squeeze this trigger—yes, the one by the grip—make sure you have a clear sight picture, and that the rifle is tucked into your shoulder pocket. You seem to be right-handed."

She adjusted the weapon on his right shoulder.

"Take a deep breath, pause, and squeeze. Do not jerk the trigger. Pull it back slowly until you feel a wall, then squeeze. Some security forces use optics, but we do not. It is important that we limit reliance on such technologies."

"Especially in a place where time is the enemy."

"Precisely, Rome."

He smiled, which made her frown, and readied his rifle.

Shoulder pocket. Sight picture. Inhale. Exhale. Pause.

Bang.

The bullet hit the target center mass, setting it in flames upon contact. An automated fire suppression system above their heads triggered. Amahle stared at the smoking target, running her hand over her face, top to bottom. Rome had seen Iwalewa execute the same motion prior. Was it a religious practice? Or tribal customs?

"You must have handled a weapon before, where you're from," Amahle said.

"I do not recall, but it feels natural."

"Hm." Amahle waited until the smoke dissipated. Rome could not help but stare at her. Her commanding ways, her laser focus, were behavioral responses that made her beauty even more expensive, exclusive. She was everything.

"Exhaust the magazine, but take your time. Practice safety."

Rome aimed down range again. A new target appeared from the ceiling, brought down by a couple of hooks.

Shoulder pocket. Sight picture. Inhale. Exhale. Pause.

Bang.

Center mass. The bullet whizzed and tore a massive hole in the target's sheet.

Bang.

Rome could not spot the bullet, but it left its chamber and hit center mass, producing a smaller hole.

Bang.

The target sizzled and crumbled like fine sands.

BANG. Bang. Bang.

Bang.

Rome slid the foregrip back and checked the ejection port. "Clear." He turned to Amahle and asked, "I have a question about the color coding."

"Yes?" She raised a brow.

"How do I determine which rounds to use? And do I load them as such?"

Amahle answered, "This is something we'll discuss during battle drills."

For the next four weeks, the two were placed in semi-isolation; they were delivered highly structured meal portions and slept on the hard floor, arms crossed over their chest. Amahle was a woman of few words, emotionless, unavailable.

Rome, on the other end of the emotional spectrum, craved a

connection, prayed for his lifelong love to open, to trust. At night, he fantasized about her surrendering to him, pouring her love into his empty vessel, with no contract.

However, Rome soon understood he was a voyager. Amahle was, potentially, a different version of his wife, in an alternate timeline he was launched into. Or maybe it was *her*, but she had been *altered* by this... *Great Fracture*. Or buried the trauma of losing him so deep she had fabricated a new reality as she washed ashore like he had.

Time was a complicated concept. During one of their rare conversations, Amahle suggested Rome was somehow another fracture in time.

"That would explain your particular affinity with death... and life. Or you could be a demon sent to annihilate my kind. We have not rooted that out yet. Get up."

Amahle held a timer in her hand. She grabbed Rome's collar from behind; the latter had his rifle on the ready, looking at the replica of a basic two-story structure.

Amahle snapped, "Go."

They both advanced towards the building. A pop-up target appeared in one of the window frames above. Rome let out a precise shot and refocused on the entrance.

A few days later, the two were running on a treadmill with fifty-pound loads on their backs.

Amahle treated the drills like a necessary formality, showing an unyielding faith. Rome had collapsed a few times, let out tears, expelled things out, momentarily lost his grip on reality, yet never openly complained. He was driven by something else other than the effective conditioning Amahle received, as she formed this militarized force of hers she called the Hive.

Inside, Rome knew what kept him going, despite his flaws

and shortcomings. He repeated it every night as he crossed his arms over his chest. A mantra.

Love you, always. At the edge of time. Love you. Always.

As the days went by, his condition improved. He was less prone to bruises, more responsive.

Footwork and studies punctuated the long days of artificial lights and curated meals. Amahle had placed an emotional barrier between the two, one Rome was careful not to breach.

But eventually, the need for closure trumped their wish for his compliance. On another night where time was an abstract notion and sunlight an obscure concept, Rome broke the imposed silence.

"I need a conversation. I want a conversation. Please."

Amahle opened her eyes to the high ceiling, arms crossed, still as the engineered night. Ambient lighting uncovered the outline of her flawless visage. Silence persisted.

"Amahle, it's important," he urged.

She sat and turned towards Rome, finding his expression was neutral, with a soupçon of benevolence. She asked, "You wish to disobey me and talk?"

"No, Amahle. I wish closure and decency."

She gauged him, fixed on the glacial eyes she could spot in the dimly-lit space. Amahle began counting on her knuckles. "Ask."

"I understand this dynamic is still new, and you've never been exposed to someone like me. But do you think I pose a threat? Have you been in love before?"

"I won't answer, and you will respect my wish. But I will tell you something else."

Rome acquiesced, "Okay."

She resumed, "In this world, men from the north have raped, pillaged. They subjected us to slavery. They broke our bones, gouged our eyes out, and asked us to *hear*. Perverted games I escaped as a child. Our own men were more protective of us but failed to stand against an entire system designed to purge our tribe from 'useless' child bearers.

"None of your fellow men delivered on their promises. On the mythos of strong providers with innate leadership. When the Hive rose to power, we took care of the murderers. But I made a promise, Rome."

"Yes?"

"To never allow my boundaries to be crossed again."

Rome challenged her. "So, you replaced a harmful patriarchy with a totalitarian matriarchy? Fighting oppression with oppression?"

Her lips curled back. "You'd never understand. Good intentions can't negate personal experience. It's about survival, safety, shelter, dignity. There may be truth in your claims, and maybe your world functions differently. You may be genuine, and wired different, but this is our reality. And that would answer your question. Now, rest, or I will break you."

One evening, Amahle spoke at dinner. "Today is our last day here. We secured more shelters for our people. It is time we meet our fate."

Rome was afraid of the prospect of another journey through time. He wondered, *Does she know fear?* She provided no clue as to whether she did or not.

Amahle left after supper, her demeanor quiet and reserved as usual. It was another unwanted separation for him, another loss after he was forced to abandon everyone he cherished for a foreign land and a shaky outcome.

Rome gave up on fighting stubborn tears. His eyes welled up as he laid on his back, arms crossed over his chest. *Why me?* Soon, the thought faded to a dreamless sleep.

And then, there was light. A parade of lab coats led by Amahle's second-in-command stormed the place in the middle of the night, fishing for a suspect.

Yehudith pointed at Rome and ordered, "Go sit. I have a few questions for you."

The survivor complied, emerging from a deep sleep, and approached the central table, where he sat. The scientists took a few steps towards him and paused.

Rome raised both hands. "No threat."

For a few seconds, they gauged his words, then proceeded. Rome was covered in sensors, wires, and patches connected to a black box placed on the table; it had no apparent switches nor display units.

Soon, it produced a chiming sound.

Yehudith sat across from him. She was definitely a killer, one with strong facial features and a raw beauty whose coldness matched her likeability, or lack thereof. She was no ally, Rome understood.

She spoke. "I will ask a series of questions. You will answer yes or no. Clear?"

Rome nodded in agreement.

"Rome, were you sent by an agency, government, tribe, or community to harm us and/or compromise our nationals?"

"No."

Silence.

"Are you responsible for the time storms we have experienced these past moons?"

"No."

"Do you know how you managed to survive the Void?"

"No."

"Do you have Amahle's best interests in mind?"

"Yes."

"Rome, do you recall your past life?"

"No." The black box chimed.

Yehudith pierced through his flesh with her slanted eyes.

"Yes. I... I only recall minor details like sensory inputs and feelings. There are triggers."

Yehudith paused and evaluated his answer in a conspiracy of silence.

The scientists were subjected to her will, waiting for her response. Finally, she said, "Run med prep on him. You have one hundred and fifty wave periods."

"Yes, Yeh," said one of the data scientists.

She left as Rome prepared for another battery of tests. His eyes followed her tall frame to an aperture in a corner. Her steps were light, the intangible pressure she applied heavy.

CHAPTER 7
LADIES AND GENTLEMEN, MR. POWELL

"MA19."

"Check."

"HAZMAT. One set."

"Check."

"Oxygen boxes. Two."

"Check."

"Check for pressure."

Rome kneeled on his tarp and reached for the oxygen bottles. They were small and lightweight, smooth to the touch, and built in a cold, metallic frame. He propped both in his right hand and used his left to turn two red valves mounted to the sides in a counterclockwise quarter turn.

Pssssssss. Rome waited a few seconds and read the barometers attached to the devices.

"6.5. Stable."

"Flashlight. TMCON One."

"Check."

"Five magazines. Thirty rounds each. Two APs. Two incendiaries. One toxin."

Rome's eyes danced over the magazines, reviewing the bullet tips through the clear coating.

"Check."

"Medkit."

"Check."

"TAC. Five units."

"Check."

Yehudith avoided Rome's inquiring gaze, focused on his layout. She concluded, "Pack and roll."

Rome, a traveler of newfound language and patterns, began packing the items that were laid out before him in a cold hangar whose bare metal frame previewed a silent war with the night.

He browsed one final mental list and sought refuge in the very same place that afforded him sanity.

Love you, always. At the edge of time. Love you. Always.

Pressed by his handler, he followed Yehudith, under close watch. Rome was a special cargo, a prisoner of the state who had been trained, not turned, to defend it. He was a foreign element with a qualifying status, a floater operating in grey areas that had never before been challenged.

Outside, Amahle was walking the ranks of a small unit. Iwalewa stood in the front, trailed by ten other bodies whose suicide mission seemed to have no impact on their resolve. Rome could hear the waves crashing afar; the outskirts of the city had an eerie quietness to it, an oppressive stillness.

The work of a heavy shadow.

He fell in line. Rome was given a clear mission, his loyalty and commitment consistently reassessed by strangers who made him the stranger. He found the conditioning drills redundant, knowing that behindhand, he was already willing to serve Amahle, to show her that his love knew no thresholds, no constraints. Would last in every life and every death.

The mystery surrounding his origins remained, but he was certain *this* Amahle was his, his intuition tussling with a complex web of timelines and worlds.

Ahead, Yehudith shouted, "Time storm!"

With Amahle, they both retrieved a small baton from their thigh holsters and planted them in the sand. Iwalewa was holding onto them, her arms locked into her children's.

The remainder of the unit, including Rome, stacked on the leaders and shouted at once, "Stacked!"

The batons produced a vacuum effect, generating ground ripples progressing inward.

Soon, a wall of glass shot from the ground up, reaching nine feet in height. The group stilled, bracing for contact. Winds rose in the cold night. Short warps rang like muffled screams.

Rome felt a hundred needles poking into the outer layers of his skin.

The first pulse swept the area.

Eyes instinctively shut. A second pulse hit shortly after.

Around the glass wall, time was twisted, and space stretched thin; it seemed that every element was blended into a composite dish that gradually built up.

A few more shockwaves reached from the front; as the wind speeds dropped, the anomaly was induced in a sleep-like quiescence.

The travelers opened their eyes, full of blurred specks.

Yehudith shouted, "Report?"

The last pathfinders in the formation tapped the shoulders in front of them, initiating a chain reaction that dominoed to the first rank.

Amahle added, "Clear." Iwalewa nodded in silence.

Yehudith checked her watch, recording a short equation on a small legal pad. A few moments later, she ordered the troops, "Next storm in ten-eighty wave periods. Chop chop!"

Her and Amahle retrieved their batons and stepped around the glass wall, followed by Iwalewa.

The remainder of the unit heeled behind, and soon, they all entered a desert of black dunes that blended seamlessly with nightfall. Strides adjusted to a running pace as the death-bringers began racing against a clock that no longer functioned properly.

The journey was of biblical consonance: the exodus of a chosen few to an uncertain fate.

Molded by Amahle at the inception, tradition dictated that the Hive traveled by foot to meet its enemies. Hard steps stamped on the coal sands, their impression camouflaged in a sea of blacks and sparkling microcrystals.

Voices rose from the dead as the unit braced for a life-altering confrontation. Amahle sang a cadence to her troops, each line resonating as her left foot hit the ground.

There is power in me!

The sisters repeated, *There is power in me, oh!*

Well beyond my body! Well beyond my body, oh!

There is power in me! Have you tapped into it, oh!

Well beyond my body! It's a mind thing, oh no!

The chants continued as if representing the energizing, rallying cry of a killing beast that moved through the shadows.

Frost settled on the sands' crystallized grains, hard to spot but evident to the touch. The cold night had pushed the warriors to change the parameters of their environmental suits and cover their faces, eyes seeking a way out behind ski masks. The singing intensified as the air grew harsher, filling their lungs with a biting dry cold.

Manisofa took me to the pit! The pit, oh! The pit, oh!

In the depths of Ma's, I found some water dripping! What was it, Hive? What was it?

It was blood purged from all the killing!

Rome was quiet, careful not to break an unspoken rule. He was following along, reminding himself of the role he played in this grand production. He pictured himself on a stage, behind closed curtains, pacing the wooden floor while Amahle sat pretty on a fake moon above head.

"It's time to spin this narrative, Ama! Oh Ama! For I shine like the sun, and you glow like the moon, yet we're both light sources. Feverish or heatless, does it matter? Is it relevant to what we have?"

Amahle replied, reading from a script, "We're both strangers to one another. It's the cycles we borrow from, coexisting but rarely interacting. You're big and bold, I'm quiet and cold. In what laws besides physics do opposites attract? It's a myth."

Rome shed tears on the stage, shaking in anger, or maybe desperation. "I will charter a course through the stars, Ama. From which I will... change. There are no riches, no titles, no fame that calls for my name."

Amahle added to the prior sentence, "You have."

Backstage, the curtains opened to a standing ovation. Rome snapped back to the present.

The night gave way to a pink sky adorned with white strokes. Temperatures rose in heat waves that distorted fields of view.

Time ran its course in the black desert, opening the sky vault to a blazing yellow sun and a purple backdrop. The weather turned less permissive, a flesh-melting heat that scorched Rome's porcelain skin; but the survivor had found comfort in his immortality, an extension of his time on Earth by her side. Pain had become a familiar friend, a traveling partner who kept the journey meaningful in its rewards.

Iwalewa was carried by Amahle and Yehudith, who had now stopped singing. The elder was shielded from the heat in her suit, her head covered by a dark headcloth.

Rome sought Amahle across the ranks, her tall frame impenetrable and unmissable, her eyes those of a seasoned killer, scanning the muddy oasis peeking beyond a dune they overcame with confidence.

She stopped at the end of the downslope, sand waves crashing the unit's feet as they came to a halt. *Gogo* was let back down, regaining balance on her thin legs.

"*Inhlamvu yesexwayiso!*"

Amahle raised a handgun and squeezed. Shots rang out, echoing in the green depression like time itself. Flocks of birds left their nests, leaves swaying under the weight transfers. Small animals ran within invisible corridors, ripples formed on the surface of a massive body of water.

Amahle looked around and shouted, "Safe. Set camp. We are twenty-seven zero-zero wave periods away."

The oasis was majestic in its radiance and vibrance. Lush greens and moist soils were colorful brush strokes on the otherwise plain canvas of the Namibian desert. Birds returned. The water stilled.

The Hive, Iwalewa, and Rome settled on the western bank. Amahle was standing by the water, looking ahead. Trees layers of various heights stood at the center of the body of water, reminiscent of a tidal swamp. A citrus aroma adorned the mesmerizing views of a lively cry surrounded by a sterile death.

Roaming guards and lookouts formed shadows leeching off the dying sun, up the steep sand slides.

Rome approached Amahle and asked, "Can we talk?"

Iwalewa and Yehudith, who had remained close, exchanged a glance as they reviewed the nearby boundaries. They walked away.

Amahle raised a hand. A few steps bridged the gap between them; they were now both contemplating the work of mother nature, lost in the patchwork of flowers, leaves, and shade trees.

"Speak," she commanded.

"How do you feel, Amahle?"

Amahle frowned at the question. "Irrelevant."

Rome dug deeper. "So, this maze we walked together. You still don't believe there was an 'us'? And Iwalewa…"

Amahle blinked, her words growing irritated. "Do you realize what's at stake? You come here, crashing on our lands with your baggage. You speak of another timeline, another world. You bring natural disasters, along with the plight of my people dying from a silent disease. It's possible *you* left us with no other option but to run to an almost certain death. Uprooting us."

Rome felt the words to be more hurtful than any hit. He let the ecosystem before him tell its story, briefly, in a narrative structure built on sounds and scents.

"This was never my intention, Amahle. I was sent here. I lost everything out there, including you! The version of you who surrendered and trusted. Our child." Rome let tears shed, looking up to the fiery skies for guidance. Amahle evaluated him.

"We both lost people," she whispered to herself.

They remained quiet for a few minutes. Birds sang their struggles, in lows and highs.

Rome realized his tactical vest would not protect him from the losses he had already sustained. He was so close to her yet so far removed.

Rome finally asked, "If we survive this… if the Dreamwalker turns out to be real… if we kill this… thing, what then?"

Amahle turned around and laid on her back, arms crossed over her chest, her frame shaded by a massive palm tree. "This is uncharted territory. Rest."

The group resumed their journey to the Void, inland. The night had considerably cooled the soil down, but the black sands they walked had absorbed plenty of heat during the past day cycle, striking a balance for a more manageable climate.

The conditions were optimal for a trek. Iwalewa was walking on her own, and the unit had spread in two staggered columns, marching the silent desert whose ground tones blended with the moonless night.

They were travelers of great significance, strong bodies and minds converging towards the root of time itself. The winds erased their footprints, as volatile as the very own world they inhabited since the *Great Fracture*.

After a few hours in a silent procession, Amahle raised a hand. The unit stopped.

Ahead, artificial structures appeared at early dawn, the sky once more purpled by a nascent burning star. Something strange laid in between the symmetrical rows of buildings before them, but Rome could not quite make out what he was seeing.

Amahle pressed a rubber pad on her shoulder strap. "Azza. Busy body!"

A voice echoed from above. Rome looked up but only found the sun he played as for his imaginary theater.

"Ama, no soft life, oh!"

All around, bodies emerged from the sands, graceful and

otherworldly. No one seemed to show concern. Rome relaxed his stance.

Sand leaked from curls and knotless braids, revealing the features of other women kings. The grains seemed to be of a different composition, leaving no residue on the warriors' hair and dark clothing.

Yehudith checked her watch, writing another small equation on a legal pad.

She added, "Administrator. No new wave, second failure."

Amahle nodded and spoke, her eyes directed at a petite frame to her right. "Azza!"

"Ama!"

"Always larger than life, oh!"

"I dey fight my own demons. Now go dey cross my lane, sister."

The unit laughed. Rome loved seeing this light-hearted facet of theirs and the genuineness of true sisterhood in display, even though the language was foreign to him.

Amahle and Azza touched foreheads together and hugged.

Azza acknowledged Iwalewa and the other sisters. "Glad you made it. We have not witnessed any storms in thirty-zero-zero wave periods. But *Òkùnkùn* is... ticking faster. Tick, tick, tick. Wetin dey happen for here?"

Amahle replied, "No sabi. But we have a guest. This is it, Azza. I no dey go back."

The two looked at Rome, who bowed to Azza. She laughed. "Rome, uh? Not everyone dey mad like Yeh." She pointed at Yehudith. "I no dey subscribe to this *white devil* narrative oh. But no more bullets tricks, okay?"

Rome felt heard. His jaw relaxed. He replied, "Yes, Azza."

Azza tilted her head in agreement and smiled. "Now Ama. When wi—"

A siren rang, heating up under the rising sun. Azza's radio beeped.

"Azza, a breach at the access! Not a drill."

Azza signaled for everyone to move forward, her group leading the charge. Weapons readied, all aimed at the strange distortion Rome spotted earlier.

The vision became clearer as they advanced. Iwalewa extended her right hand forward, her palm facing the oddity. Rome held his handgun at the low ready, careful not to capture any friendly in his line of sight.

The anomaly was unlike anything he had ever been exposed to, even as an outsider spit out by a foreign timeline; one who cheated death.

Through the strange sighting ahead, an invisible wall of heatless waves, a reflection of the outpost's structures materialized in a never-ending, recursive upside-down vision.

A Droste effect.

The group came to a halt a few feet away from the Void's access. Azza approached it alone.

A shape breached through, setting foot in the outside world.

The man was tall, his tight curls bringing volume to a bushy beard. His dark skin glowed in the sun. An expensive-looking pin-striped suit complimented his athletic frame.

He raised his arms, waving like a charismatic preacher, smiling at the rifles that welcomed his arrival.

Azza shouted, "Stop. State your name!"

The man swept Azza's flesh with piercing eyes and laughed. He began clapping, the sounds reverberating through the space.

Finally, he said, "Ladies and gentlemen, Mr. Powell."

CHAPTER 8
HAS ANYONE EVER RETURNED?

"Child, he's well-groomed like the *Eye*. Walked through the columns of time, cheating death, like your foreigner. But he is no Rome. I sense no struggle in his eyes, Ama. No love."

Iwalewa paused. Mr. Powell let out a soft laugh.

She resumed, "There's duplicity. He's not to trust. A new kind of *tokoloshe* gouged out the eyes of a corpse."

Iwalewa raised a hand, her lean muscles stressed by a taxing attempt to *see*. Her eyes rolled inside her closed lids as she looked beyond the physical plane.

Mr. Powell waved her away. "*Gogo*, you know there is nothing to fear. You are wise, no? Let me speak before you make a judgment."

Iwalewa reopened her eyes and sought Amahle. The elder motioned *no*.

Mr. Powell seemed uninterested in the theatrics, addressing Amahle directly.

"I came to guide your people, Amahle." He then turned to Rome, peering through the unit's diamond-shaped formation.

"And pledge allegiance to your soulmate, the one who survived time." He pointed at the survivor. "Yes, you."

Rome made his way through the crowd. "How do you know about us?"

"I've seen a thousand lives in thousands of universes. I know the math will not make sense to you, but it is beyond your comprehension, no offense. And I know this particular version of yourselves was a couple, before this... unfortunate series of events."

Mr. Powell extended an arm to the Void.

"But less of the past, more of the future! Have we decided on a route?"

Weapons loaded, producing a menacing, staggered mechanical sound. Amahle asked, "Stranger, why would I trust you?"

Mr. Powell turned around and ran his spiderlike fingers through the Void's barrier; a clear liquid slipped through his extremities. He turned back towards the trained weapons and joined his hands together.

"Amahle, you already know. Plus, well, I was sent to serve you. I'm bound. I cannot go back unless it's with you. And him."

Amahle raised a hand and inquired, "Who sent you? And what do you know about the Void?"

Mr. Powell clapped again. "Ama. I am no tool for evil forces, no catalyst, no enemy. I am simply... useful." He paused and smiled wide. His warmth was either genuine or skillfully deceptive. "The Void? *Òkùnkùn*. New Ajegunle. La mise en abyme. Countless names from the timelines I've ventured into. In this world, it appeared after the 'Great Fracture'".

Mr. Powell approached Rome. "And you might be the key."

Iwalewa shouted, "Enough! Amahle, *uku*." The two exchanged a silent conversation.

After a few seconds of tensed reflection, Amahle shouted, "*Uku!*"

Rome leaped back. Shots fired at a rapid rate, dumping shell casings on the sandy grounds. None reached their target, Mr. Powell, instead crumbling in fine sands like a firework of dust.

The man in a suit smacked his teeth and stood still.

He drawled, "I understand. It is not my place to judge. Iwalewa, you may have reserves. It's okay. I'm here to make sure you cross that veil safely, so you can realize your fate. Whatever that is."

The weapons were still smoking. Amahle shielded Iwalewa and demanded, "Why would I follow you, with your tricks?"

Mr. Powell pointed at Rome and looked beyond the unit. "Let me answer with a question, Ama. Forgive the theatrics, but this is the best way to put it. Has anyone ever returned from a fracture? Besides us two, here."

Amahle remained silent.

Mr. Powell clapped and resumed, "Great. Let's get to it then." He crossed the threshold to *Òkùnkùn* and disappeared within the mists.

Rome approached Amahle, who was still shielding Iwalewa.

He asked, "How likely are we to survive without him?"

She stared into Rome's soul, looking for a hint of his intentions. For a few tense moments, she remained silent.

Giant birds flew over the outpost, clouding the shapes below. Eyes raised to the skies, following the avians' flight trajectory. Amahle finally looked at Azza and said, "I dey go *Òkùnkùn.*"

Azza nodded in agreement, scanning her outpost. "I sabi."

Amahle began suiting up, retrieving another black neoprene suit from her tactical backpack, one whose fabric was thicker, coated with a matte finish.

Others followed. Rome understood the implications and started gearing up himself, readying for a secret war.

Sophisticated oxygen masks turned the explorers into stranger things, creatures from another plane whose eyes were concealed by tinted lenses. They checked each other's circuits and manometers, and all raised a thumb.

Amahle checked Iwalewa's gear and held her face, with a gentle touch.

She said, "*Gogo*, I trust your judgment. But there's a chance we can fix this fracture, open the world. This is something you wanted."

Iwalewa nodded and held Amahle's hands. "Promise me you won't let anything corrupt us, Ama."

"I promise, *Gogo*."

After a few bits of quiet reflection, Amahle's Hive moved forward, merging with the strange kaleidoscope of upside-down worlds that was the Void.

Azza waved at her people. Shots rang in the air, announcing the beginning of a world-altering quest, at the crossing of realities.

CHAPTER 9
JANGOLOVA

Golden dust swept across a herringboned pavement. Above the hissing oxygen circuits of Amahle's Hive, metal structures hung upside down in the skies. Ahead, massive sinkholes spun red sands whose particles were sucked into an infinite vacuum. An emergent layer of a canopy shaped like a pit of snakes neighbored the sinkholes.

The place was a deconstructed fantasy, a dreamworld that knew no boundaries, abided to no code.

The result was grandiose. Amahle processed the picture, the challenges it could pose. To mankind, this was a terrifying concept challenging the already controversial notion of reality.

Mr. Powell had already left and was seen entering a massive dust storm a mile away, past the red wormholes.

Amahle's voice came through the group's radio channel, muffled and almost drowning in a sea of strange cries. "Azza would have said, 'I thank God I godly'."

A few of the warriors laughed. The words triggered a reaction in Rome, a chain of flashes from a foreign past. He was still as the night.

Amahle continued, "Let's spre—"

"Oluwa na him comfort me." The words slipped out of Rome's mouth, as if sung by a native to Azza's lands.

Amahle exclaimed, "How do you know this?"

Rome directed his tinted lenses at her. His piercing eyes could be felt if not seen.

"There was this song we played, from a place we both loved. Our wedding song. It was beautiful... The melody escapes me, but..."

Amahle and Rome stared at each other; looks were concealed yet *received*.

She returned to the wildlands and readjusted her gear. "Okay." The dust storm Powell entered inched closer. "Let's... spread our signature. Rome and *Gogo* are staying with me. I want you paired in complementary skillsets, TOs and CAs. CQB and Marksmanship. Or engineering. This... Mr. Powell already left, and I still have reserves, but it seems like this cloud of dust is the only way forward."

The unit quickly moved its members around, rearranging the pieces of a complex puzzle.

Amahle shouted, "*Asihambe*! Watch your steps."

Rome followed Amahle and Iwalewa as they walked the cobblestones and quickly transitioned to red sands of an inexplicable hardness, their feet bouncing back on the concrete-like texture.

Amahle's rifle scanned the sector, sweeping a broad radius. The snake-like plants swarmed closer and closer as the group carefully approached the lamenting sinkholes.

Iwalewa's black lenses found Rome. She said, "You're different, child. If Oluwa's name brings you comfort, you may still have good left in you. But there's this thing lingering in your soul... Something dark, chaotic, unconventional. There's a Mr. Powell in there."

Iwalewa refocused on her steps. Rome felt a profound respect for the elderly woman, like he was programmed to but could not quite explain why. He remained silent.

Amahle came to a halt. The visibility still allowed others to notice. They followed suit.

She crouched and ran a small flashlight over the plants intertwined in a complex pattern of hooks and twists. No movement. She pulled a knife and stabbed one of the stems. No response.

Amahle rose and raised her hand. "*Asihambe!*"

The group resumed their advance, stepping on the soft parterre of greens. To their sides, ghosts were calling from the underground of bottomless pits. The dust storm continued its advance on them, massive yet surprisingly gentle.

In the skies, something shrieked with desperation. All weapons raised towards the upside-down metal structures overhead.

Another sound added to the complicated layering.

Tick. Tick. Tick. There was no visible threat, however.

Rome found the structures familiar: the reflective windows, the speared ends, the massive heights...

Something scraping. *A scraper?* he wondered.

Tick. Tick. Tick. TICK. Gravity was reversed in a loud swoosh.

Something swept beneath the travelers, throwing them on their backs, precipitated into a heart-dropping pull towards the artificial buildings. Rome felt his airways retracting under the pressure. He began pulling on his mask but quickly stopped, regaining a semblance of control over his motor skills; his eyes were burning, pulsing in their sockets.

T t t t t t t.

Bodies had left the earth, set on a collision path with the celestial vault. Heat built up within the suits, traversing their padded layers like an electric current. The world turned loud, warning the travelers with a deep, deafening sound.

Suddenly, gravity reverted to its prior state. The group was pulled towards the red sands again, obscured by the dust-charged winds expelled from the incoming storm.

Rome blinked, and the picture turned sharper: Amahle, with her distinctive shoulder structure, was somewhere to his left, or maybe right, holding another smaller shape. Some of the others had fainted, their bodies free-falling in a grotesque display.

A voice came through the radio. "Find your sist... The shock absorb..."

Rome recognized the deeper tone and chopped speech. *Yehudith's.* Something about shock.

The suit.

Rome tapped the rubber pad mounted to his shoulder strap three times; his suit inflated, and a small parachute deployed. Around, more parachutes appeared in the sky, bringing volume to the flattened silhouettes dropping to their potential demise.

Ten seconds.

Rome guided his glide to intercept Amahle. She was conscious and her suit inflated, yet she was repeatedly slamming Iwalewa's rubber pad as well as her own.

Her voice came through the radio, chopped in bits. "Get... sist... Parac... Failure... Honor."

As they prepared to hit the ground in full force, Rome caught them and shielded the two from the fall. His parachute snapped and flew away.

"Ama, trus..." His tone was measured, decisive in its straightforwardness.

Amahle relaxed and held Iwalewa tight, balling in a smaller

visual signature. Rome grabbed the two and found his balance as they entered a raging dust storm that had gained coverage. They braced for impact, lost in uncharted territories.

Boom.

The ground was softer than expected, but Rome's organs still imploded, punctured upon impact, absorbing most of the deadly blunt force a body set on a crash course from one mile above would sustain. Amahle and Iwalewa barreled further down, spraying sand in their wake.

Inside the storm cloud, winds were raging, loud and corrosive. Amahle, fighting not to black out, reached for *Gogo*'s band and pressed on it; Iwalewa's vitals were stable.

Rome. Yeh.

She lifted Iwalewa up, fighting a sharp pain in her sides, and made her way back to the point of impact, following fading tracks.

A body appeared to her left, fading in: one of her sisters in arms. A ripped canopy was covering her face.

Amahle desperately tried the radio, "Anyone?!"

No response.

She put Iwalewa down and crawled towards the casualty, lowering her center of gravity to withstand the wind gusts more effectively. Her hands detangled her sister's parachute cords. She retrieved a knife to cut the cords individually. The parachute flew in the wind, flapping its artificial wings.

The sister's vitals were low. Amahle checked the integrity of the casualty's equipment and removed her mask to identify any potential obstruction to her airways.

She looked back at Iwalewa, who was sliding on the sand, dragged by an invisible force. Amahle ran back to the elder and tied her to her wrist with silicone-like handcuffs. She returned to the injured, fighting the pull from *Gogo*'s dead weight.

"Anyone?"

No response from the radio.

Amahle struck the casualty's plexus with swiftness. Her sister began convulsing, gasping for air. Her eyes were dilated, swinging left and right as they sought Amahle's face. The latter reapplied the oxygen mask on her sister, pinning her body down to the ground while pulling Iwalewa closer.

"Iso! Fight it!"

The sister's body began stabilizing. Her fingers were digging into the sands, her muscles tensed and defined. She took one more shot at finding a buried anchor and got a hold of herself.

Pandemonium broke out, hitting the barrier of sound. Amahle raised a thumb to her sister's lenses; she reciprocated. The Hive's leader felt relief.

Rome.

He had saved her and *Gogo* from a gruesome death, his bones crushed in the maneuver. The surviving sister, Iso, helped Amahle pull Iwalewa, still unconscious, preserved by the oxygen intake from her suit.

They both carried her deeper into the storm, following the dying marks leading to the epicenter of the crash site.

Rome's body was there, crooked into submission. His thoracic cage was expanding and retracting, threatening to burst out of his smoking suit. His ventilation circuit and mask seemed intact. Amahle ran to him and instinctively grabbed his hand in a display of affection she was not acquainted with. Her sister remained behind, holding Iwalewa straight.

The loud winds and whispers still prevented the group from communicating verbally. Amahle laid a hand on Rome's chest; his breathing slowed down to a more manageable pattern.

Visibility had worsened; the survivors were now shadows

grazed by sands. Amahle locked in on her sister and pointed at a direction to her right. The sister raised her free arm.

Amahle lifted Rome from the ground and followed Iso and Iwalewa, all leaning forward to outlive the roaring winds. There was no sign of Mr. Powell, no other traces of life.

In this confused, Martian-like landscape, survival was the most volatile element.

After a few minutes of an excruciating march, Rome partly regained his range of motion, walking assisted.

The dust storm began clearing, leaving room for a pathway flanked by string lights connecting a nexus of magical trees. Behind them, something struck chords of a divine sound. A harp. The chords reversed, in a stretched warp.

Amahle found the parallel with the time storms unsettling. She clicked.

"Go, go, go!" she shouted.

Her group picked up the pace, running through the covered pathway whose dense canopy blocked the skies from penetrating. Ahead, a small lake reflected a starry celestial vault. The world around had switched to a night cycle.

"Jump in!"

The harp sound faded away, its last reversed note booming through the shifting dreamworld.

Rome, Amahle, Iso, and a semi-conscious Iwalewa dashed to the lakefront and dove in, breaching the lake's surface. In this cold, dark place, strength laid in numbers. The group stacked together, sweeping the murky waters for potential predators.

Soon, they froze, blending in with the dark.

Atop the surface, a vacuum effect produced an eerie sound borrowed from the earlier sinkholes, causing ripples to replicate in a chain reaction. Amahle began sweeping her surroundings again, familiarizing herself with the low-visibility environment.

Above, the whispers ceased. The vacuum was no longer felt through the body of water, the ripples grown faint. Below, the silhouettes of silent watchers maneuvered in slow motion.

Finally, the group emerged from the depths.

The pathway they ran was no longer. On this side of the lake, the edge poured into nothingness, serving a deceitful perspective. On the other end of the expanse of water, an A-frame cabin with a glass façade revealed an open concept in which a silhouette teased its mysterious outline.

Amahle looked around and spotted more shapes emerging off the lake's depths. She shouted, "Yeh?!"

"Ama!"

Amahle relieved Iso of her protection duty and grabbed Iwalewa, still in a semi-comatose state; the elder's oxygen apparatus produced a stable breathing pattern, yet she was still unresponsive.

Iso began swimming towards the shapes that claimed to be her sisters. Rome assisted Amahle with Iwalewa, covering her sectors of fire and shielding the two from others.

They waited a bit longer, floating in this dark, cold space.

Iso shouted, "This is Yeh, Ama!"

The trio swam furiously to the survivors, disrupting the lake's dynamics.

Yehudith's face was uncovered and partially burnt; flakey wounds ran ravenously from her chin to her nose bridge. Five other sisters had outlived the gravity storms.

Amahle processed their losses. *Two.*

She pointed at the cabin and ordered, "The house. There's someone. Tread lightly."

CHAPTER 10

THERE IS SOMETHING. IT HAS PRINTS

"You know what she's capable of. What she's done for us. *The greatest of the great.* We need to jump start her vitals, Yeh," Amahle reminded her sister.

Iwalewa was on her back, set down on a wooden deck whose creaking matched her irregular breathing. Her wearable respiratory device followed the same erratic arrangement.

Yehudith welled up in tears that were not tied to the prospect of losing their *Gogo*; her burn injuries had taken her to new thresholds of pain, ones her body could no longer contain. She wiped her tears and blinked, stretching her jawline.

"Here. This should work." Yeh gave Amahle an auto-injector. The latter reviewed the small syringe, a black device with a display unit.

"Vasopressin?" Amahle asked.

"Yes, Administrator. It's a prototype, an improved formula."

Amahle nodded in agreement and stuck Iwalewa in the fleshy portion of her outer thigh. Rome and the other sisters guarded the improvised tactical field care, scanning the cabin and the dense jungle closing in on the structure.

The deck began shaking; Iwalewa was convulsing, inhabited by violent tremors.

Amahle pinned her down and removed her oxygen mask, racing against an imaginary clock. She turned her *Gogo*'s face sideways to expel the white foam from her crooked mouth.

Iwalewa's eyes were frozen in time, stunned by suggested visions of terror. As time made its advance, her body grew still and quiet: then, she returned to the land of the living. She gasped, writhing, "Ahh—"

Amahle pressed a firm hand against the aging woman's mouth and whispered, "Shh. This is me, *Gogo*. Your child of the sun. You're alive."

The elder fought pain in a muffled struggle, rapidly blinking and shifting sights. A few night birds took off from nearby tree lines.

"Shh. *Gogo*. You're alive," repeated Amahle.

Iwalewa began nodding. The injection's entry point on her tactical suit shrunk on its own, until her gear's fabric fully reconstructed. Amahle handed the auto-injector back to Yeh and investigated Iwalewa's evasive eyes, waiting for them to find balance once more.

The elder relaxed. "Child... the sun."

Amahle smiled and replied, "Yes."

Iwalewa looked around, seeking the stars reflecting upon the lake. She asked, "What happened?"

Amahle sat her straight as Yeh began checking her vitals and frame.

"We crashed, *Gogo*. The pale flesh saved us. Then Yeh brought you back to life."

Iwalewa reached for Yehudith's face in a display of affection. The latter showed no emotion. "What happened to your face, child?"

Yehudith answered, resuming her check-up, "Crashed too, *Gogo*. Any dizziness?"

Iwalewa looked into Yeh's eyes, searching for buried feelings. "No, Yeh. I'm fine. Thank you."

She stood slowly, taking deep breaths to overcome the madness of her rebirth, and retrieved her self-contained breathing apparatus, placing it on her tired features. Soon, her voice reemerged through the internal comms.

Facing the white man, she said, "Rome, thank you. Maybe you're not lost after all."

He turned around and found Iwalewa's black lenses; they both nodded to a common understanding.

The Hive, a swarm of murder hornets, began gliding on the hard surface of the extended deck.

Their movements were now precise, synchronized, fluid, like shifty wind streams under the mesmerizing influence of the Coriolis effect. Amahle led the assault on the A-frame cabin whose lights drew a pathway on the pier they had set foot on.

Water drops from their wet suits further darkened the light woods whose irregularities gave the docks a carefully curated vintage look. Behind Amahle, Iwalewa, Rome, Yehudith, and the Hive survivors tilted their weapons at a forty-five-degree angle, seeking blind spots and hot walls through the massive glass pane of the modern-style retreat.

Sharp, dark faces danced on the reflective surface. The man inside had his back turned away from the entrance, his arms casually set on the edge of an expensive-looking sectional.

Amahle raised a hand as she approached the entryway, tapping its frame's edges.

She whispered, "No heat point. Powell's toying oh."

She relaxed her shoulders and twisted the door's handle.

Click.

The Hive flooded the space, their complex footwork leading to the brown suit and tan pants.

Mr. Powell, indeed.

"Great," he simply stated, raising a hand.

The survivors' tactical gear instantly dried, regaining their structural integrity. Yehudith's burnt skin layers bonded to sustain new, regenerated cells. She pressed on her remade skin, testing its elasticity.

Outside, rain began pouring.

Iwalewa waved the performance away and carefully approached the man in a suit. She laid a hand on his forehead, pushing it back against the sofa's plush fabric. Mr. Powell's juvenile eyes widened as he found himself paralyzed, looking for Iwalewa in his peripheral vision but never quite finding her shape.

She moved closer to his ear and hissed, "You will reconsider toying with my children, hm?"

The elder's hand found his jaw line and turned his head to the side so he could see her menacing lenses. She maintained eye contact with him, establishing dominance over his incapacitated body.

Amahle dispatched her unit to the furthest corners of the spacious living space. Rome remained by her side, his handgun pointed at Mr. Powell's chest.

Iwalewa sought fear in the stranger's eyes, the acknowledgment of a verbal contract.

She asked again, "Do I make myself clear?" then released her hold on him.

Powell reached for his satin collar and pulled to relieve an invisible pressure. "Okay, okay!" He readjusted his sports coat. "I have no control over this construct, this dreamworld. I can shape a few things and pull a few strings, but *this* madness you went through... this isn't of *my* doing."

Iwalewa replied, "Then you can certainly share my children's burden. Unless..." Her voice held a hint of warning.

Mr. Powell looked around, making brief eye contact with the Hive members, and stopped at Rome.

He finally capitulated. "No, please. That's enough. I'll share."

Rome looked at the two. There was a conspiracy of silence, an unspoken agreement between the wise and the mischievous.

Mr. Powell resumed, "You exercise free will, right? I was just waiting for you all." He pointed at the back of the cabin and stood. As he began walking the massive space, the remainder of the group converged towards him, their oxygen masks hissing in the eerie quietness of the cozy retreat.

Iwalewa approached Yehudith and placed a hand on her heart. "Yeh, child, I know he healed you, but beware of false prophets. They often hide behind a single deed. Self-preservation."

Yehudith remained quiet and nodded in agreement. They joined the formation trailing behind Mr. Powell.

Outside of the back window, sands of different shades and tones crashed into the glass in a roaring Song of Dunes.

Waves.

Beyond the sea of dust, the darkness housed a pulsing sound.

Mr. Powell interrupted the contemplation. "Can you hear it? Sand waves. Shockwaves. And then, there is something. It has prints." Without further notice, he opened the backdoor to the right of the glass frame and entered the night.

The others stacked on Amahle and tensed, snapping at every pivot.

Yehudith's voice was preceded by a short static. A slight reverb was applied to it as it came through the Hive's internal comms. "Comms are up. No hardware issues. There may be further disturbance oh. Oxygen at forty/ten. We have a backup charge each."

Amahle answered, "Loud and clear, Yeh. Sisters?"

The remainder of the Hive shouted in unison, "Loud and clear!"

"*Gogo?*"

"Yes, precious."

"Rome?"

Rome was quiet, staring at the sand waves passing through his legs.

"Rome?" she pressed.

"Yes, I can hear. Thank you."

Mr. Powell was waiting for the group, visibly annoyed. He waved at Rome dismissively and shouted at Amahle, "This one loves you. Ha! Shall we?"

Amahle stole a brief glance at Rome and nodded in agreement.

The sands felt heavy. The explorers advanced in the dark, leaning against the current, pushing one another forward.

Above, the skies were fractured into billions of shards, bright light vessels whose shine never resolved the low visibility on ground level. This world would not obey the laws of physics, nor subject itself to mankind's reassuring constructs.

It was wild and unpredictable, disorderly, fear-inducing, yet somehow... magical.

Then it struck, unannounced. A whizzing sound flew by Amahle's ears; she could feel the heat through her thermal layers.

She clicked. "Bullets!"

Suddenly, more projectiles rained from above, piercing one of the sisters' flesh like thin paper. Her black lenses turned to her pack before she collapsed.

Amahle shouted, "Move! APs!"

The sister was lifeless, unresponsive, gunned down unceremoniously. Yehudith dragged her bloodied body across the sand waves, rushing forward with the group. The deadly rain of Fender bullets strings followed them, swarming to its next targets.

Mr. Powell, who had watched the scene unfold with concern, raised a hand; the bullets exploded in a fine dust before reaching their targets, covering them in blinding sands.

He shouted, "That's all I can do for now! Watch yourselves!"

Amahle rushed forward, carrying Iwalewa; the file formation stretched under her fast cadence. The crackles of the bullets intensified, their loud pops disorienting in their erratic frequencies. Ahead, deep footprints had survived the wavy sea, immutable and eternal.

They led to edgeless faces staring into the pitch-black night. *Demons.*

Rome broke formation, shielding Amahle. He fired shots, breaking the fragile truce between this world and its visitors' instruments of death. More shots rang out, fired by the edgeless enemies whose eyes glowed a harrowing red.

Tracer bullets ignited the night, piercing Rome's flesh. He fired back, unsteady.

Amahle held him as they pushed forward. He muttered words in his dying breath, sounds lost in the detonations and loud sand waves.

Rome managed to speak up, dragged further out by Amahle, who also fired back.

"Use me, my..." A crack in his voice foreshadowed his thousandth death.

This time around, Amahle hoped for another resurrection; she no longer feared nor rebuked him.

She shouted, her voice combating the brewing storm, the fate of her tribe hanging in the balance, "Stack on me. Fire at a forty-five! *Gogo*, behind me!"

The file formation tightened up as Amahle slowed down, sheltered by Rome's upper body, shells grazing his ripped suit. Mr. Powell veered right to a downslope and disappeared.

The unit continued forward, fighting a strong current while chasing the *tokoloshes* away.

The firefight was an exercise in reciprocity. Tracer rounds lit up in the dark like deadly spells.

The muzzle flashes of Amahle's fighting force blinked at a higher rate, decimating the dozens of faceless beings lurking in the blanket of an eternal night. Rome jerked under the impact of lethal weapons handled by creatures made in nightmares, like a ragdoll swayed by a rough handling.

The knee-level waves widened, distorted like the static of an equipment on the frisk. Voices reached from under the waterless sea, in hushed tones.

Shh, baba. THEY'RE DYING.

All at once, the ground sunk and precipitated the group's descent into an endless abyss.

At this very moment, Amahle thought, *There won't be enough Romes to save us all.* She held onto his lifeless body, fulfilling an unspoken promise. Amidst the chaos, Amahle cried out for Iwalewa, hoping she would pick her voice through the whirlwind of dust and rocks.

"Love you, *Gogo!*"

Gravity interrupted the fall. The fine and coarse particles

reverted their course, sucked into an invisible vacuum shooting upwards. Amahle and her group hit a hard ground that materialized under their feet.

She realized this world was toying with them, operating in total impunity. Was Mr. Powell truthful when he admitted he could not control all variables?

She let a word out, in the stillness of a vast silo. "*Jangolova.*"

Around her, the sisters were tending to a body. Amahle was trying to understand why.

She was holding one herself; a man whose pale complexion stood out among the darker skin tones present. Why was she holding him? An elder was there, too. *Young enough to be mobile, still.* The benevolent matriarchal figure approached Amahle and laid a hand on her forehead. The latter did not feel the need to push her away or argue the outcome.

"Amahle," the elder sang.

The dots connected at a furious rate. Time launched forward.

It was Rome in her arms, the man who often sacrificed without careful consideration.

And Iwalewa, *Gogo*, a counteragent to toxic impulses and deadly sins.

The sisters, who committed to this suicide mission with an unwavering loyalty.

Mr. Powell, who may after all be more than just a mischievous god. Or spirit.

The sisters. *The sisters.*

Amahle set Rome down. He entered another painful cycle: the deadly shells' purge from his being, the closing of his wounds.

She ran to her sisters. Yehudith was tending to a motionless body whose eyes had lost the spark that was life. The sister was gone.

Amahle looked at Yehudith and ordered, "She will be left on this battlefield, offered to her *Gamab*'s village."

Yeh nodded in agreement as the group stepped away from the corpse, running their hands over their faces.

A cry for help sent frightening notes to the circumambient cylindrical structure, bouncing off the concrete curves of the tall silo. The sisters turned around; Rome was fighting strong tonic spasms, writhing in pain on the cold floor, semi-conscious.

Amahle returned to him and crouched. She found his elusive eyes and whispered, "Thank you. You're no longer a *tokoloshe*. Now, fight."

CHAPTER 11
"DID YOU KNOW TIME WAS A MONSTER?"

"What is this place?"

"*Nomkhubulwane.*"

"The shapeshifter? Nothing new."

"It's different here. You no longer fight space itself. You bend time."

Mr. Powell's fingers moved frantically, like the baton of a classically trained conductor.

Amahle had led her tribe outside of the silo, into the unknown. Heat waves rose from the unusually glossy concrete coating the grounds.

There was an urban concentration, with wide pedestrian streets and tall structures whose spires were lost in a radiating glare. Further out, serpentines and rolling hills had drifted from the kingdom of God, gorgeous in their complexity and verticality. Each building had a custom access and lobby, forging strong narratives carved in stones, marbles, and noble woods.

It was all and nothing; it was sterile yet exciting, complex and nonetheless basic.

Powell added, "This bears a close likeness with the very idea of *Òkùnkùn*. Seemingly absurd, self-contradictory yet real."

Rome interjected, "A paradox."

"Precisely." He nodded.

So many shapes and textures yet no sound, no biome. Amahle surveyed the street, now a smaller artery running through an overpass. There was still no sign of life, no organic elements aside from the wood framings. The entire city was a bland yet well-structured dish cooked under a focused heat.

Amahle ordered, "Let's move faster. Oxygen is at twenty-five to five with a backup charge."

The sisters acknowledged with a *oh!* Amahle shifted to Iwalewa and Rome, who in turn nodded in agreement. The latter was quiet, and sickly.

He's gone through so much. To what avail? she thought.

The oxygen tanks and the suit continued walking the boundless metropolis, specks in a sea of metals and concretes.

Mr. Powell, who had previously waited ahead, approached Amahle, falling into step with her pace. His face was devoid of the playful smirk he once adorned.

"From what I understand, there will be timelines, Ama, iterations of you and others. They will converge towards what you're looking for. I'm not sure how, however."

Amahle continued forward, silent, fighting exhaustion and dissociation, crossing on a tightrope with one single stabilizer: her environmental suit. Her sisters looked no better, but they were all bound by a sacred promise: to overcome.

She did not understand Mr. Powell's statement. In her recovering mind, questions sieged the stronghold that was her conscience.

Iterations of me. Others?

Are they hostile?

How will they show?

How long until we find the Dreamwalker?

What will happen next?

The thoughts accompanied a quiet march in this sinister landscape.

The buildings' proportions were epic. Rome *felt* he had never seen *this* done to that scale, and Amahle was completely foreign to this configuration.

She felt lost in this space, unwilling to seek guidance from the unreliable Powell and the cold streets of this hellish place. There was no movement, no tracks, no clues as to where to look. She needed something, an edge in this silent war. *A vantage point.*

Amahle stopped and looked up. The sisters readied their weapons, confused.

"Nah oh." She pointed at one of the structures and asked Mr. Powell, "Do they have rooftop access?"

Mr. Powell glanced up and replied, "Most, yes."

"Okay. Let's go."

Amahle walked to a set of revolving doors to her right and entered the lobby.

The hallway was, inexplicably, out of place. The modern, minimalist architectural print remained, but there were clocks, devices of all shapes and sizes placed on the walls and the high ceiling.

They were out of synch with one another, producing a vertigo-inducing noise pattern.

Tick. Ti--Tick.

Tick. T t t t tock. Tick. T tick.

Amahle ordered, "Cut your sound. We're going dark."

The sisters and Rome pushed a button on their masks. Iwalewa waited a few seconds, touched the ground, and pushed hers.

Amahle activated her own noise-cancellation. The walls turned quiet, her feet substituting her ears; Yeh's technology provided great relief, allowing her to reconnect with her current reality. Life flowed through a narrower stream and a less tortuous path. Colors and lines appeared more vivid, enriched with details best appreciated seen and touched.

Amahle sought the building's elevator and found a lift hidden behind a faux wall.

The shaft was big enough to accommodate the group, bar handles circling a grey flooring. They entered the silver structure, stacking on each other as tightly as possible to establish a safe distance between them and the door.

Amahle pushed a button labeled *P*, the highest of them all. The door closed.

The leader raised a hand and pointed at her right ear; the unit deactivated their noise-cancellation, reacclimating to a subtle, droning sound.

Amahle's voice flooded the radio channel. "Okay. We need a vantage point. I hope to find access up there. We need to scout the entire sector for any anomaly. Tears in the fabric of reality, movements, shadows, travel patterns. You know the drill."

They all patiently waited for the elevator to stop—stern, unspeaking, and focused. Rome looked around, realizing how Amahle's people had thrived in her greatness, how the radiance of her rich soul and her creative leadership shone a bright light on the world like a beacon of hope.

At this very moment, his love for her knew no bounds; he was certain her sisters felt the same.

He murmured, "Amahle, look at them. We followed you to the edge of the world. You're nothing short of a blessing."

She stole a brief sidelong glance at Rome. Yehudith probed

on his flesh with her optics, her tinted lenses sending accusatory looks. Iwalewa tapped Amahle's shoulder twice.

The doors opened. At the end of a narrow hallway whose walls bore no doors, upward steps were carved in stone, oddly rough and raw.

Amahle engaged first, her weapon aimed at an access point up the small set of stairs.

As she closed the gap, tension rose, the distance shortening by the steps, the pressure from incoming findings felt beforehand. She checked the door's metal frame for traps and heat points before pushing onward.

Blinding lights. Like the immaterial blades of bright whites.

Amahle looked down, her sight recovering on a darker shade of grey. She walked a few more steps and turned to Rome, who had been relatively quiet up until this point. Nonetheless, his consistency in behavior and service forced admiration.

For a fugitive moment, she thought of this maze they walked together, and this child the other Amahle may have carried. As she ran the flowery walls with him, she felt admittedly whole. Softened, even... Loved?

She directed her attention towards the skylines, as the picture became clearer and the black specks in her vision now turned into dizzying views of an urban nightmare. The temperatures had climbed even higher, invisible conduits of hot air blowing from the streets below. The city was synthetic in its grid-like patterns and reflective skyscrapers.

No soul has ever blessed those constructions, Amahle thought.

"Prep the site. Set a three-sixty surveillance," she ordered.

The sisters began moving around the rooftop, retrieving equipment from their tactical backpacks. Pieces were placed on a massive chessboard.

Amahle resumed, "Set your suits to cooling mode. We'll let it run for twelve-hundred wave periods."

Rome and Iwalewa complied, standing by Amahle in the middle of the roof, studying this quiet world.

The suits began regulating their body temperatures, giving the survivors a newfound sense of clarity. Mr. Powell was on the edge of the skyscraper's crown, hanging on the ledge, visibly unbothered.

"Any visual?" Amahle asked.

Yehudith answered the radio call, "No, Administrator."

The all-around quietness Amahle felt was oppressive to her. She understood they could never go back to *Jangolova*, could not retrace their every step.

What was the alternative? This world did not speak to her.

She looked at the horizon, seeking a break in patterns, the emergence of a new biosystem, a disruption. Her environmental readings still indicated the air was unbreathable; the unit's primary oxygen tanks were running low, adding to growing concerns no one dared express.

Amahle established eye contact with Mr. Powell. She felt like he could see through her lenses, his juvenile eyes interrogating her soul.

She inquired, "How do w—"

Without warning, a loud hissing struck the rooftop. Dust rose in an invisible tunnel cutting through the terrace. A face materialized, and its body followed.

Her cheeks were stretched by a honeycomb-like layer of skin, akin to that of sea creatures with gills. The outer layer was breathing on its own, expanding and retracting to the beat of the dust blasts. Her complexion was dark, with a reddish undertone. Wild curls lent volume to her sharp nose bridge and almond-shaped eyes. The stranger wore no tactical equipment, nor did she rely on respiratory assistance; she was wearing a robe, her frail silhouette swaying in a self-contained storm.

Despite the alien nature of her mutated anatomy, most recognized the posture, the main features, the elusive beauty...

Rome said, "Is this... a version of you, Ama?"

Amahle had difficulties processing the sight of another her, a version stripped of her refinement, ridden of her inhibitions. She was looking at a feral animal, an uncomfortable possibility.

Amahle-2 looked afraid, uneasy. Maybe it was the strangers spectating through a magnifying glass, or maybe the existence of another *her*. She sought refuge in the shelter of her timeline, in the cover of a quiet, caged storm.

Amahle approached the invisible corridor. Her counterpart averted her gaze.

Seemingly absurd and self-contradictory, yet well-founded and true. A paradox? Precisely.

Amahle continued, reaching for the quiet whirlpool inside the imperceptible tunnel. She paused and looked in the direction her more primitive form had sought, then inched closer.

Amahle-2 refocused on Amahle and waved her away, jumping up and down in desperation.

But desperation was a common disease, and Amahle was out of leads. No one dared interrupt the first contact. Mr. Powell was eyeing Amahle with an amused curiosity.

As her hand entered the immaterial corridor, all hell broke loose.

Galaxies and clusters infiltrated Amahle's bloodstream, multiple realities flashing before her eyes.

She was God. She was *her*. And *her*. And *them*. Her legs ran a closed loop until *something* launched her into the next spiral. And the next coil. And the next helix.

She was given different skills with each transition, borrowed from various features, her mind framed in boxes of several shapes. Amahle transformed into a hardened feminist on the picket line, a nihilist in a meditation room, a traditional housewife on a manicured lawn, a dictator on a superyacht, a serial killer in an evidence storage... Time mishandled her, toying with Amahle like she was a disposable doll of interchangeable outfits.

All at once, she imploded into an infinity of particles. Now, she could see it all. Scattered across the universe, she felt the burning desire to locate her counterpart.

BOOM.

Amahle-2 was there, contemplating the exclusive beauty embodied by a unique network of misty pillars. The tall geological formations blended in with a lush rainforest producing a light fog.

The two were perched on the highest peak, surveying the land from a thirteen thousand feet elevation. There were no fears, no wild variables, no unknown parameters. They were gods meddling with this Earth, in total control of a world that existed both outside and within.

Amahle-2 spoke in a foreign language her counterpart somehow understood.

She told Amahle, "J'avais peur des conséquences. Mais nous sommes là, maintenant."

Amahle replied, "Ton visage, ta posture... Ton monde, a quoi ressemble-t-il?"

"Je suis un produit de mon environnement, Ama. Je viens d'un monde façonné par la peur, poussée par un instinct de survie. Tres peu ont survécu l'implosion de la mise en abyme."

"Combien sont morts?"

"Huit... milliards."

A silence settled, short-lived in the buzzing ecosystem.

Amahle-2 resumed, "Mais tu as Rome. Et après avoir exploré des centaines de mondes, c'est la première fois que je le vois entrer un autre espace-temps. Le mien est mort."

Amahled inquired, "Donc... Rome est la clé?"

"Possible. Protéges le, quelque soit le coût," implored *Amahle-2*.

Her last words rolled into a collapsing funnel. Amahle was pulled into a vacuum, snatched from the mountain range by a higher god. She had now returned to the Void and the vantage point she had conquered seconds prior to her interaction with her alternate.

A few miles overhead, a massive dust wave had appeared, ever-expanding. It began descending on the group, creeping like the feared monsters of folktales.

Amahle-2 and her self-contained timeline were no longer.

Alongside the corridors of the city's furthest corners, giant structures began crumbling like sandcastles, faster and faster as the dust storm above precipitated its own takeover.

An invisible yet tangible pressure grew stronger on the tactical suits, coarse grains scratching the virtually impenetrable material.

Afar, the buildings kept caving at a faster rate, wiping entire perimeters out.

Amahle realized the destruction carried a pattern: *It* was headed towards them.

"EVACUATE THE BUILDING. FILE LINE!" she shouted, waving at the rooftop access.

The unit began fleeing the scene, with Iwalewa carried into the stairwell firsthand.

Rome caught Amahle's lenses and shouted, "I go last! Less risks!"

Amahle nodded, following her sisters downstairs. The walls began shaking as they rushed into the narrow escalier.

"Hurry!" Yehudith shouted as she carried Iwalewa, zooming through.

The file line snaked through the turns, shifting their own weight to offset the violent swaying of the building. There were fifteen more floors between them and the lobby.

Above, a deafening sound shattered the structure with a low, deep bass.

Rome looked up and yelled, "It's collaps—"

The group sped up, stretching their burning lungs.

The fifth floor. Yehudith was widening the gap between her and the rest of the formation, reaching incredible speeds. Behind, the sisters, along with Amahle and Rome, extended their strides, preparing to cross over an imaginary threshold.

As darkness poured from above, the unit reached the lobby; its nascent light was suffocating in the hands of a wrathful dust storm booming outside, as well as the blanket of the structure's sequential demolition overhead.

The unit shot through the massive hallway they first entered and proceeded through the exit.

Amahle and Rome followed last. The doors stopped revolving as they rushed in, trapping the two in between panes. *Ama* pulled her gun and shot all four corners of the glass before her, shielding her face. Rome had backed against the next door pane, turning away from the shots.

She kicked the shattered glass and rushed outside with Rome. Her sisters were blurry shadows fading into the calamity that had landed on ground level. They ran away from the collapsing skyscraper, ignoring muscle failure and the weight of their equipment. The characteristic hissing of their oxygen circuits was lost in the surrounding wind gusts rocking the crumbling city.

Together, they dashed towards the remaining Hive and Iwalewa, hoping to outpace the raging monster that was Time.

Soon, they disappeared, swallowed in the all-around chaos.

CHAPTER 12
"NA LIKE CLAY, ABI?"

"Ama!"

"*Gogo!*"

"Sisters!"

"Powell?"

"Here."

The tailored suit of the supernatural guide grew sharper in the commotion. Mr. Powell grabbed Yehudith's shoulder and pulled her closer in a fathering gesture.

"The others?" she asked, shouting.

"They are somewhere out there." He pointed at the eye of a storm, one bordered by a giant wall made of sand.

Yehudith rushed towards the barrier, fearless and decisive. Mr. Powell motioned a rotation with a pristine, manicured hand that had never suffered the shortcomings of humanity. In turn, the Hive commander involuntarily retraced her steps, rewound through a disobedient iteration of time.

"Wait, Yeh. Iwalewa is closer. And so are the remainder of your sisters. Which ones should you prioritize? *Them,* or a man who can cheat death and a woman who has won all of her wars? They need you. You are essential to this. Remember?"

Yehudith squinted through her lenses to gauge Powell's sincerity.

His face bore no malice. His eyes were steady, and his speech was measured.

She looked around, seeing more structures had collapsed. Their metallic framing shook the grounds of the wide street, whose earthy tones reminisced a gateway to Hell. There was no sign of life around. An earth-shattering buzzing sound accompanied the low-pitched slap of a deadly wind.

Yehudith bent to counteract its effect.

"HOW DO I FIND THEM?"

Mr. Powell looked up to an ambitious structure downsizing in real time a mile away. "You have to regain visibility, Yeh. Reclaim this madness."

Yehudith thought of it, deconstructing the very basic concepts of this world. *Òkùnkùn*, the Darkness. The place where things changed.

Changed. Change.

Changing?

She muttered to herself, "Ama said time was a monster." She asked Powell, "What did you say about time, when we first arrived here?"

Mr. Powell stood next to her, shielding her from some of the wind blows that assaulted her flank. He tilted his head. "Pardon?"

Yehudith shouted, her voice cracking from the prospect of an imminent death, "ABOUT SPACE AND TIME!"

"You no longer fight the space, you bend time."

Yehudith, a world class engineer, understood the implications. Time was a monster, a living thing, not a scientific process. It was no longer relative, as they thought. It followed its own arbitrary rules, showed a temperament.

Like the *street japas*, the children with no fathers, it *reacted*.

She sat down and took a deep breath, looking at the world through her bulletproof lenses. Powell smiled.

Ama never thought this through, instead establishing contact with another timeline with no precautionary measure. Acting like the white devil, impulsive and unrestricted.

She dispelled the thoughts, looking for hope and acceptance, fishing for positive feelings in the muddy pond of her complicated mind. Back home, Yehudith led those children, those slum boys whose internalized fears rendered misguided.

Here, Time needed to be understood, heard, and respected. It was territorial and disarmed by its own complexity.

A paradox.

She closed her eyes and slowed her breathing down, reminiscing about her younger years training by Amahle's side. The storm still raged, but the blows and gusts grew irregular, less threatening. She felt Mr. Powell's hand on her shoulder.

Bunny chow, bunny chow.

I chooned Ama once.

This mal loud but I chowed.

I chooned Gogo once.

Yebo I will bow.

When the time comes.

I chooned Ama once.

Yehudith continued singing, louder and louder, as the collapsing structures became fewer and the noise levels lower.

This mal loud but I chowed.

I chooned Gogo twice. It's lonely at the top.

She found peace, seeking refuge in an elusive childhood she was quickly robbed from.

Her eyes opened anew. The dust had settled, opening her line of sight to an apocalyptic cityscape. Some farther areas were still battling their own demons, experiencing short-lived visions of strange voyagers crossing invisible paths. Other time travelers.

Yehudith stood, swatting Powell's hand away. "Sisters!"

Her voice echoed through the fractured alleyways and avenues. She had asserted dominance over this difficult child, finally.

The japa may not mind a few warning shots.

She raised her rifle to the skies and issued three of said shots. The high velocity rounds challenged the quiet of this hellish maze.

No response.

Yehudith checked her oxygen reserves, finding her tank had depleted quicker, running at a low thirteen percent. Her brain resorted to complex calculations, in pursuit of a bridge to an effective countermeasure, a potential way out.

She issued two more warning shots and listened for a response. To her right, something barely audible erupted, muffled in the distance.

Another gunshot, maybe.

She began rushing towards the source, issuing a few more shots as she covered a mile.

Another response came forth this one sharper and baring the same deep bass to it.

My sisters.

She ran faster, ignoring her screaming pains, driven by the end goal. Around her, a thousand pictures burst in rapid succession, giving the desolated cityscape a thousand faces. It was a bustling marketplace, an overcrowded jail, the Zen sounds of suspended gardens and waterfalls.

It was all and nothing. Everything, everywhere, all at once.

She asked Mr. Powell, who casually ran by her side, his suit impeccably mounted on his flawless frame, "Am I hallucinating?"

"No, Yeh. Time is talking to you. Time knows you're special. And so do I."

She continued, squeezing the trigger once more, the shell casings sinking in the sands.

Bang.

The sound was loud, a distinctive feature of the Hive's weaponry. Ahead, a few heads peeked around the corner of a dilapidated skyscraper, an unfinished sculpture, a skeleton of steel in a glass cage.

She ran towards the group, her weapon pointed at the unknowns.

They reciprocated, rushing her position.

"Yeh!"

Yehudith recognized the inflexions, the postures, the firearms handling techniques, their thumb over bore. She lowered her weapon.

"Yes. Sister?"

"Eish, yes!"

Yehudith immediately thought of the woman they all shared their DNA with.

"Where is *Gogo*?" she demanded.

Among the small crowd, a shorter silhouette made its way to the front.

This female pointed at the shifting landscapes in the nearby perimeters. "Na like clay, Abi?"

Yehudith found comfort in her presence, in Iwalewa's immutable wisdom and selfless nature. Iwalewa stole a brief glance at Mr. Powell, her eyes unreadable behind her glazed lenses. He smiled.

She asked Yehudith, "Where is your Administrator? And the traveler?"

"I had to choose, *Gogo*. I chose you."

Iwalewa raised a finger and ran it across her mask. She said, "We have to find them. Where did you see them last, *mafungwase*?"

Yehudith pointed at a distressed area in the far distance, one beyond an observable wall of brown dust and raging thunders.

The sisters approached. Yehudith raised a hand.

"We need a line. We need to shift to a rope team. You!" She pointed at a sister flanking Iwalewa. "Hook us up!"

Yehudith stood in front of the procession, still and tensed, her weapon raised at the storm taunting them ahead. She addressed Mr. Powell while maintaining her sight picture.

"Powell. There must be other timelines converging towards them, correct?"

"Most likely, yes." The man in a suit was casually pacing, indifferent to the surrounding chaos.

A sister raised her voice, exercising dominance over the warped whispers and shrieks reaching from the storm before them. "Yeh, we are hooked!"

"Good. Take your spacing."

The group stretched longer, leaving thirty feet gaps between members. The objective was over a mile ahead yet the nightmarish sounds of a hundred crying souls felt immediate and close.

The sandy grounds cracked under Yehudith's first steps; it thickened and blended, no longer slipping through fingers and soles creases. It turned cold and heavy, offering fewer energy returns.

The reddish undertones shifted to reflective whites.

Snow.

"Turn your cooling off. The suits should retain your body heat for a few wave periods. *Gogo*, how are you?"

She waved her forward. "I'm okay. Go on, child."

Yehudith kept pushing, her legs fighting the natural pull of the full snow. On all sides, the metallic structures of the urban concentration shapeshifted into mountain ranges and ridges, a bewildering array of rock formations.

The dust storm that was ahead remained, however; it had survived this wrinkle in time.

Footprints set on the ice, leading to a curtain of browns spilling over the immaculate grounds.

Yehudith stopped and studied the supernatural phenomenon. The haunting voices coming from beyond had lowered and strengthened their argument, as if aware of the group's presence.

Yeh remembered the rooftop incident. The tower decaying. The revolving doors. The dash to a nearby street that had shielded her from death. The dust particles swallowing the world. Iwalewa escaping.

The inception. When the Administrator meddled with the other timeline's affairs.

Yehudith spoke to the rest of the unit. "Let's sit. We can no longer interact with those... timelines. The Administrator will find us."

She looked at Mr. Powell, who concealed his playfulness behind a semi-grave expression.

He remained standing there while the others sat on the stained snow.

Inside the storm, chaos ensued. Rome pulled on Amahle's rope twice; she stopped and turned around. Shadows flew over the fractured sky, demons driven by an insatiable hunger. Hundreds of Amahle's iterations roamed the space, passing by them, denoting different behaviors, walks, postures and showcasing slight physical alterations.

Rome was not present in these neighboring worlds and alternate universes; he drew interest from the other Amahles, who physically reached out for him but could never quite touch him or integrate his world.

They were caught in time loops, prisoners of eternal damnation as they offered the overall setting terrified expressions.

He gently pressed his Amahle's arms as she approached in an affectionate gesture. "The inception. On the rooftop. It all started when you reached out to your counterpart. How do we find our way out?"

Amahle asked, brows furrowed, "How?"

"Stability."

"Rome, I... There's... There's nothing I would love more but this is a foreign concept in *Òkùnkùn*." Rome held onto her, fighting invisible pulls. She resumed, "Unless..."

"Yes?" Rome asked.

"Unless we promote something other than movement. Unless we stop and do... nothing. Unless... we refuse to see."

Rome released his gentle hold and stood before her. He inquired, "What do you have in mind?"

Amahle looked down and shouted, "Let's sit! And hold onto each other. The proximity will prevent them from passing through us. You seem to be immune to their reach!"

Rome nodded in agreement as he sat with Amahle, holding

her hands. They both looked down, ignoring the horrifying visions of this faraway plane.

Rome added, "If we survive this, what's next for us? Will you give me a chance?"

Amahle squeezed his hands. "I don't know. I came to fix this world, as well as others. I don't know."

They remained silent, the shadows of shadows towering over the grounds they focused on.

Rome ran his thumbs along Amahle's rugged hands. The hardness of her skin was foreign to him, but the act itself allowed his struggling mind to find comfort in a distant past. "Ama?"

"Yes?" she answered.

"This is all familiar to me. Something we used to do. Sit and bond, shielded from the craziness of the world. Suspended in time."

The two clicked. The skies began clearing while the shadows faded.

Amahle lowered her voice. "This may be how we survive it. Matching your timeline. I see no other Romes, so you may be a… constant? In some shape or form."

Rome kept his head down, his steely eyes locked on the queen.

"We may have a chance," Amahle whispered.

Beneath them, the ground had shifted textures, grown hard and cold.

For a short moment, Rome and Amahle were made blind by the reverberation of a new sun on the white snow; the setting reminded Rome of those cold seasons spent with his loves, celebrating the strange yet beautiful creature that was life.

Amahle spoke. "The lenses won't filter all the light. Take your time."

"Have you seen this before? Snow?" Rome murmured.

"Yes. The reunification wars up north. And my sole purpose there was…"

"To feel whole," he finished for her.

The two remained silent as the weather cleared, coming to a mind-bending conclusion.

Somewhere around, footsteps repeatedly died in the snow, brought back to life in a muffled cry. Amahle stood and raised her rifle, looking for potential targets reaching from this bright landscape.

Her vision adjusted to dark shapes. Tinted lenses.

Closed ventilation circuits uttered a hissing sound.

"Sisters?"

"Administrator?"

CHAPTER 13
THE DEAD PEOPLE MUST GRIEVE

The Hive stood before Amahle and Rome in the vastness of the glacier.

"Administrator?" the first individual asked, running a hand across their mask.

"Yeh?"

"In the flesh."

Amahle found Yehudith's shoulders. She looked beyond her sister, sweeping the remainder of the unit with her concealed, dark gaze. Rome stood and approached.

"Sister, who are you carrying?" Amahle pointed at a fighter holding a lifeless body.

"Bimi, Administrator."

"Will you take her further?"

"Yes, Administrator. Until the waves wash."

An elegant olive-green double-breasted blazer materialized on the glacier, with the flesh of a being reassembled by the sun itself.

Amahle passed Yehudith and walked the procession, nodding at a distinctively small individual.

She stopped by Mr. Powell and asked, "Where is—"

Gunshots rang behind her, thundering in the emptiness of this barren world. Amahle pivoted and raised her rifle, quickly identifying the source: Rome.

"What are you doing?!" yelled Amahle.

Yehudith raised her hands, masking the barrel that was pointed at her.

"She tried to attack me. I issued warning shots." Rome lowered his gun.

Winds crashed in waves, obstructing the sunny skies with the occasional dark cloud.

Amahle demanded, "Yeh. Speak."

The sunlight quickly faded. Yehudith lowered her hands. "This white devil triggered an extinction-level event. How many sisters have we lost since he crashed upon our shores? How many, Ama?"

Rome argued the claim, "I was stripped away of everything, everyone I loved, uprooted. Have you thought of the sacrifices I had to make? The challenges I've faced? That I still accept death, even though it's terrifying, so you can live? Does the color of my skin trump the harshness of my condition? Does it make it all go away, magically?"

Amahle looked at the two, their emotions guarded behind their mask, and a false sense of control.

Yehudith seethed, "You have never fought our wars. You are weak and fragile, driven by volatile emotions. An impurity among our kind. And you poisoned her!" She pointed at Amahle.

The winds grew louder, forming serpentines of snow dust sweeping down the glacier.

Amahle lowered her rifle and struck Yehudith's neck; she

grabbed her throat with the confidence of an apex predator, pinning her down, her massive frame sinking in the soft ice.

"This is the last time you will question my loyalty, sister. Remember the butcher of Nairobi? Do not test me."

The woman struggled to speak. "Yes, A... dministrator."

Amahle stood and fired three shots in the air, exercising dominance over Yeh.

"Sisters, are we in agreement?"

The others raised their right hand.

"Stand up, Yeh. Powell?"

Mr. Powell approached the front of the procession, looking at Yehudith's snow-covered suit with amusement. He refrained from smiling further as he felt Amahle's tinted lenses gauging his suit. "Yes?"

"Where to?" Amahle asked.

The blizzard had lost some of its intensity, fighting the sun's sudden rise to power.

"It is not where, my friend. It's when," Powell explained. "What have you learned from your journey through time thus far?"

Amahle sized him up, then looked down the infinite glacier. Ahead, a snowy ramp plunged into the gargantuan mouth of a bottomless abyss.

She spoke, appreciating the vertigo-inducing perspective. "To never intersect with another timeline. To follow Rome. There are no alternate versions of him, at least none we witnessed."

The sisters nodded. Yehudith remained still.

Mr. Powell looked at the tired travelers and smiled. "Indeed. I think Rome exists outside of this construct, like me, but in a different manner. Rome, I have a question."

Rome relaxed and stepped forward. "Yes?"

"Do you ever sleep?"

"Pardon me?"

"Do you ever fall asleep?"

Rome paused. He looked at the sisters. And Iwalewa. She nodded, encouraging him to answer the question.

"No," he said finally.

The silence grew louder. Amahle ordered her sisters, "Hook us to your line."

Mr. Powell laughed and added, "Rome. You and I, we are… dark, twisted fantasies. The occasional guides. Unwilling messengers, maybe. Live your truth. Embrace it."

Amahle ignored Powell and hooked herself onto Rome's carabiner clip. "We'll follow, Rome."

"Understood," he replied.

The rope team and the dead sister began their journey downslope, as the sun shone brighter and brighter.

Transient voyagers and timelines ascended and descended the glacier, alternate versions of Amahle, Iwalewa, and the Hive sisters. Rome shifted their trajectory and weight at every encounter, slaloming through a complex web of unseen poles and gates.

The unit was quiet, focused on averting collisions with other worlds. However, Amahle noticed that some postures turned asymmetrical, and a few limbs twitched, all concealed and shameful.

Exhaustion.

As they pursued their trek, the setting remained unchanged, infinite, eternal. Snow extended along the downslope to no variation.

Rome stopped.

"There is no point. It's a loop."

He surveyed the glacier and unhooked himself. "Please, wait here."

Rome headed left to the edge of the glacier. Down below, a fine mist formed an emergent layer, as if they had reached the space above the clouds.

Rome's thoughts wandered in this expanse of cotton balls, his mind slipping through the mesh of miniature liquid droplets, frozen crystals, and other particles suspended in the atmosphere.

Death, or continuous torment? For him, the latter was the only option. For those he loved, a more permanent outcome would present itself.

In the end, continuing down this glacier, the eternal fate of villains a la Dante's Inferno, would only bring suffering and agony, while this world would crumble, unresolved.

He turned around and walked back towards Amahle. His hands found the oxygen apparatus he removed, his eyes struggling to adjust to the brightness.

A few seconds passed.

"I'm... going... going to jump, Ama. I may... never... return so, p... lease allow me. See... me."

He opened his arms, fighting tremors. She let him in, sizing up the extent of his love through the gentle embrace and the light squeezes.

Amahle asked, "Why?"

"This... may solve... dilemma. We... lost. There... m... ight be... path." Rome had more and more difficulty breathing with each passing second. His skin quickly adopted a bluish-purple hue.

Amahle reminisced about the conversation she'd had with her alternate, standing on top of otherworldly pillars planted in a dense rainforest, all-powerful in her design. She remembered the state of omniscience, the knowledge flowing through God particles...

I must trust his judgment.

Rome took one last look at her as she hid her eyes behind layers of a literal and figurative mask.

Her radiating browns sun warmed with inner gold. Perfection.

"I lo… you, A…ma. Alw… will."

Rome let her go, donned his mask, and sought Iwalewa. For a few seconds, quietness allowed for his struggled breathing to find more stable patterns. He fought to articulate, "Thank you, *Gogo*. Thank you for bringing us together. Sisters."

Most acknowledged. Rome turned around and ran past the edge, jumping off to the unknown.

As Rome plunged to a deadly fall, he made peace with the cards he was dealt with.

There was beauty in his fate, in being reunited with the woman he longed for, in cheating death to prolong her life. He was whole, content.

Rome closed his eyes and relaxed his muscles. He tapped into the incomplete memories of *his* Amahle: her complexity, her beauty, the vulnerability she displayed, the feminine energy she embraced in various fashions.

In the world he had crashed, she was tougher, chiseled by the burden of her status.

However, he still recognized some of *his* Amahle's core traits; across all timelines, they shared a particular sensibility for mankind's condition, for its needs and pains.

Whether a leader or a partner, she was still the woman he would give up the world for.

Thank you, he expressed to a higher power.

His frame hit a hard ground with full force, bouncing off to various points in space. Bones shattered in his damaged body, his organs obliterated by the sheer force of the collision.

And then, the world stopped.

Amahle peeked over the edge Rome conquered. His embrace was genuine, almost... comforting.

There was something embodied and claimed in his displays of affection, something that was never felt prior.

And now, he's gone, Amahle thought, unsure of how she truly felt, deep behind the fortress of her conditioned mind.

The Administrator somberly returned to her pack, hooking herself back up.

"Together, sisters."

As they resumed their descent, the cold grounds sent small vibrations underfoot. Suddenly, snow dust sifted through a vacuum that filtered out the smaller particles. The soil hardened under the defining transformation.

"Halt!" Amahle shouted as they stacked on each other, shielding Iwalewa.

The world leveled to a flat field. The natural light from the sky vault surrendered to a darker soil and an unruly canopy dying to cast its shadow. There were warped whispers crazed in deconstructed speeches, words Amahle could not quite comprehend.

The temperatures rose, a blasting heatwave sizzling on the surface of giant Kudzu leaves.

"Unhook!" Amahle ordered.

The unit executed and stretched out in a file formation. One of the last sisters walked the line to retrieve the rope; she rolled it and stuffed it in her tactical backpack, her movements stacking against the emergence of a new world.

"Standby." The earth beneath had achieved its final form, but the voices remained—chaotic and desperate.

Amahle broke formation and swept the unit's sectors of fire, running a circle around her Hive. There was a path to another downslope; her rifle ignored the passage to scour the surrounding jungle.

Sssssss. Another set of prints appeared, like the ones Powell spoke briefly of in the sea of sands. *The faceless?*

The marks were shaped like a breeze blowing through the vegetation, forming on an unmarked pathway. Amahle raised an arm, and the remainder of the unit lined up behind her.

A light tap on her shoulder triggered her steps, measured and purposeful. She was wondering if the voices were the products of a collective hallucination or her own; the sisters were sleep deprived, operating beyond mankind's known limits. The time inversions, the shifting landscapes, the witnessing of alternate selves... It was a wild sensory input that flooded the gates of their consciousness unchecked.

The prints soon evaporated, leaving room for a dead silence. They had supported a well-orchestrated performance leading to one single outcome: the uncovering of a body.

Grass blades impaled his porcelain skin like a fungi parasite, but his sharp features and slick black hair had survived his entrapment. He was buried in a green sarcophagus, turned into an object of study at the hands of the murderous Mr. Time.

Amahle dropped and started digging below, uprooting his frame and bringing his scarred flesh closer to hers. She whispered in his ear, brushing his skin off.

"Please. You still owe me answers. And we owe you our lives."

Mr. Powell reappeared then, triggering the usual set of rifles that were upset at his ways.

Amahle whispered once more, "Please, Rome."

For the first time in her life, she was no longer in control of her emotions. Something more powerful had taken hold. Tears welled up in her eyes as the fear of losing him creeped in.

His environmental suit was torn to shreds, but his bones and tissue were preserved, reassembled in an awkward composition. At this very moment, Amahle was hoping someone could assist, maybe reaffirm that death was still a foreign concept for Rome.

Oh!

His body twitched, tensing in her embrace. Tears ran along his cheekbones, his eyes dancing under lids that were struck by frantic tremors. He was in pain, fighting to reemerge.

Amahle lifted him up and carried him to a clear patch of dirt, closer to her sisters. "*Gogo*, I need you."

Iwalewa's slim frame approached Amahle and asked, "Yes, child?"

Amahle whispered, "I'm scared." Rome's body was still battling an invisible illness, consumed by the fever of a thousand suns.

Iwalewa took Amahle's hands and squeezed. "Good, Ama."

The sisters circled around the foreigner who gradually became their accomplice, with the exception of the one carrying her dead counterpart. Rome's nails dug the ground as he recovered a broader range of motion. He was alive, breathing to the beat of his struggling lungs.

Iwalewa crouched down and ran her fingers along his facial features, from his hair to his chin. "Stop," she said.

Rome came to a full stop, obedient, his eyes seeking a hidden sun. Above their heads, the green vault had smothered the skies.

But Rome was paralyzed, working through a gruesome resurrection.

Amahle had noticed his breathing, but intrusive thoughts took precedence over operational details.

She clicked.

"Yeh. Is the air breathable?" Yehudith tapped a pad on her chest.

She answered, "Yes, Administrator."

Amahle looked at Powell. "Where are we?"

Mr. Powell took a few steps towards her and looked around. "The neutral zone."

"Tell me more."

"It's a... it's the endgame. The heart of what you call *Òkùnkùn*. Time dies here, where the Dreamwalker lays dormant." He pointed at Rome, who was fighting to regain control. "He may be the wild card."

Amahle slowly processed the information. *Time dies here.*

"Powell. Why are we still standing then?"

"You come from the past. Most of the dying timelines here come from the future. Plus, you have Rome."

"What about you? Are you exclusive to this timeline?"

Mr. Powell smiled. "It's complicated."

Iwalewa interjected and raised a hand. "Ama, child, do not listen to his wicked tongue. Follow your own path."

Amahle wished she could see through her *Gogo*'s eyes.

I could.

"Okay. Everyone, take off your suits and pack up. We're going light tac. Chop chop!" She pointed at the sister carrying the dead and smacked her teeth. "Lay Bimi down."

The unit executed the order, docile. The sisters lost a layer of clothing and packed their environmental suits in their tactical backpacks. Amahle took a deep breath and enjoyed the flawed air of a natural system, regaining a semblance of humanity.

She looked at her sisters, her grandmother, and the stranger who became thicker than blood; her eyes rediscovered their quirks and features, the emotions they painted or concealed.

The timing suggested hope: the transformative power of Rome's countless sacrifices, Yehudith's lesson in humility, Iwalewa's spiritual protection... Actions that led to this very moment, the final chapter of a timeless journey.

"Sisters, weapons check!" Amahle ordered, her mind landing on more practical grounds.

The rifles clicked in one synchronized block. She turned back to Rome, who was now sitting up in the dry dirt, trying to make sense of his newfound life.

Amahle approached and said, "Welcome back. You saved us. Again."

In an unusual public display of affection, she placed her hand on his stained cheek; he placed his over.

"Thank you," he murmured.

Amahle stood back up. "Good. Sisters, we are setting camp here. Forty-eight-zero-zero wave periods. I will take the first watch, for twenty-four-zero-zero. Yeh, you'll set up a flatbed above ground. But first, Bimi."

Amahle walked towards the Hive's casualty of war. Rome followed, aided by Iwalewa. The sisters converged towards the dead body, which was carefully placed on a bed of Kudzu leaves.

One by one, they ran a hand over her discolored face. Rome and Mr. Powell remained in the back, attentive. Powell whispered, "Those who died here will cease to exist, Rome. In all timelines."

Amahle touched the casualty last and looked at her sisters.

"As *uMvelinqangi* arose from beneath and His messengers

returned from the moon, death became a reality. And although we breathe of perishable blood and flesh, we have held life to the highest standards, cheating death even before Time crashed upon our shores. The Hive is an institution, the celebration of resiliency, conditioning, and excellence. The highest echelon, the missing link between humans and gods. And for this very reason, we will not be subjected to victimhood but instead trample the Earth in power."

The sisters began stomping the soil.

"We will celebrate the sacrifices of our sisters and rejoice in their strength and selflessness. Bimi, Kana, Alewa, Johannes. May you take our fight to the Kingdom, pleading our case to *uZivelele*, he who is of himself."

She paused. Yehudith laid her eyes on Amahle, deeply focused on her shoulders' frame.

"*Asihambe!*" Amahle resumed.

The sisters shouted in unison, "*Asihambe!*"

Amahle continued, "Now, we let the dead people grieve."

CHAPTER 14

"IT FOLLOWS IN THE DARK. BLENDS IN WITH THE LIGHT."

Rome sits across from me, lounging on a chaise. His reading glasses, I must say, clash with his sportsy looks, but it works. He's deeply invested in this novel; something about an American zoo.

To my left, a massive park is entrapped within a grid of tall buildings and connecting avenues. But this is no longer Nomkhubulwane. This cityscape is vibrant and colorful, full of life. There are cars and people woven into the patchwork of a formidable hive.

It is high up in this ivory tower, north of the 50th floor maybe. But here, I feel safe. The outside visual buzz gives the impression it is noisy, disorderly. But here, it is quiet and structured.

I want to savor this moment and let the vision come to fruition. There's a burning desire to understand...

How can this man possibly protect me? The Administrator. The woman who won wars. This foreign world has me acting equally foreign, however. I do not bear scars; I do not bear the burden of leading a nation. I simply exist, living a new purpose under the leadership of a man who never once had to demand it. He is gentle *yet purposeful, culturally sensible yet fearless. He is mine, and I am his.*

"Imani. Spotted," Rome muttered, still living within the pages of his book.

This beautiful young lady to my right... She rushes from another room and hugs me tightly.

The outpouring of love is... unmatched. She shares his facial structure and my darker complexion, her smile a happy disease, contagious and unstoppable.

I want to talk, but I can't.

I'm a spectator riding along an elaborate scene.

She disintegrates like a sand statue losing its binding, slipping through my fingers. The sun sets and the city lights shut off. This room feels more like a stronghold now, a strategic position. Something reminiscent of my world. Or the other world. Or one of the other worlds.

My sisters enter the room. Somehow, Rome is gone. They warn me of a ruthless monster that dances on the waves. And then all crumble.

I'm alone.

Amahle opened her eyes to the midnight sun of the neutral zone. Rome and Mr. Powell were posted by the pathway she had not yet engaged in.

Tick... Tick... Beep.

The sisters woke up almost instantly, checking their gear and jotting notes on remaining reserves and logistical details.

As the bodies stretched, the stomachs filled up, and the weapons reloaded, Amahle approached Rome and Powell. The latter was counting on his fingers, backwards, from ten. She and Rome sustained a silent conversation, as if they shared a long-lost memory.

Finally, Amahle asked, "Are we ready?"

The two quietly agreed.

She turned around and shouted, "*Asihambe!*"

The Hive and Iwalewa gathered around their Administrator, Rome, and Powell.

"*Gogo*, how are you?" Amahle inquired.

Iwalewa ran a hand over her wrinkles and smiled. She locked eyes with Powell. "Welcoming any outcome, child. I'm well."

Amahle acquiesced, "Good. Yeh, are we clear?"

Yehudith, shoulders raised, head slightly tilted upwards, answered, "Yes, Administrator."

"Good, good. Let's move, sisters. The end is near, past a few wave periods."

Strong legs stomped the ground. Bodies straightened, anticipating death with a smile.

The group set foot on a downward slope, sheltered from the sun by another arched vault of prolific greens. Light was filtered out by a developing canopy that seemed to grow on sight.

The trek was peaceful, the world still. An ecosystem made itself known to its visitors, no longer shifty and paranoid. To Amahle, this tonal shift foreshadowed something worse, however. She remembered sharing the same feeling before her final push for the reunification of the northerners and her people.

"Stay sharp, sisters! This world isn't yours."

Mr. Powell added, "Yours, not *ours*? Interesting word choice."

Amahle declined to comment. Ahead, perspectives shifted again. The sky was still concealed under a green dome yet fought to light up sections of a surreal landscape whose deep sinkholes harbored virgin biomes.

Amahle came to a halt, studying the edge of a massive pit covered in various shades of mosses and trees. Wild grass blades grew on its steep sides like untamed hair. Down below, strange creatures inhabited those worlds within worlds, gauging the visitors before fleeing the scene.

Along the sinkhole's vertical sides lay a path carved in the rocky formation, spiraling down to the shadowy depths.

Amahle raised a hand. "Powell?"

"The answers to your most pressing questions? They await down there."

"Yeh." Yehudith approached the edge.

Amahle resumed, "I need a recon."

Yehudith raised a hand and waved it. Another sister came and opened Yeh's tactical backpack. She retrieved a grey ball vacuum-sealed in clear plastic. Yehudith was given the unassuming object, the sister taking a few steps back with the others. Rome and Amahle followed suit. Mr. Powell stayed closer, peering curiously over Yeh's shoulders.

On a section of the plastic seal, a red label protruded from its surface. Yehudith peeled the label off.

"Three. Two. One. Mark." She threw the ball high in the air, in a flawless vertical.

The plastic quickly expanded, taking the shape of a small reaper drone. The unmanned aircraft instantly ignited its small propulsion engine in a soft hiss. The plastic dissolved.

Yehudith ordered, "Zoya, I need a thermal analysis on this sinkhole. Entry. Exponential. Forty-five to ninety degrees. Repeat command."

The drone, hovering above the unit, flashed some lights on its wings. "Thermal analysis. Entry. Exponential. Forty-five to ninety degrees. Confirm?" a synthetic voice inquired through the unit's internal comms.

"Confirmed," Yehudith answered.

The reaper drone began its incursion into uncharted territory, plunging into the depression, swift and silent. Amahle and her sisters surveyed the land, looking for potential traps and hostile activity within the hole's perimeter.

The rainforest below was complex in its layout, unpredictable in its patterns. From the sparkling moss to the crooked trees and fine capillaries running wild on rocky grounds, there was beauty in the chaos.

Yet more camouflaged predators.

Amahle hoped to find the answers to the *Great Fracture* here, and an elucidation of Rome's origins.

Would *this* be her last moments with her tribe, before Time healed? Before the infinite numbers of worlds birthed by shattered timelines were sucked into the vacuum of a massive reset?

She looked at her sisters, quiet and impenetrable.

They were trained well, maybe too well, she thought.

The absence of a catalyst like Rome from their lives, someone they may have been deeply involved with in a distant world, led her to believe they were unable to fully appreciate the tipping point of this journey, the pivotal threshold they were now crossing.

Yehudith interrupted the thoughts. "Administrator."

"Yes?" Her attention snapped to the woman.

"I have my readings here." Yehudith had retrieved a small screen from her tactical vest.

The drone resurfaced from the darkness, quiet. It ended its course above their heads, awaiting further instructions.

Yeh resumed, "There were lifeforms detected but nothing significant in size or behavior. The sinkhole is nine thousand feet deep. The path carved within the sides is structurally sound. There is another junction on ground level, leading to unidentified structures."

Amahle asked, "Oxygenation?"

"Acceptable."

Satisfied, she nodded. "Okay."

Amahle glanced down below, evaluating their tactical options. She looked at Yehudith.

"Yeh, we're going in with air support. Be prepared for anything. That sonic countermeasure? Use it if needed. I will rope down while you lead the rest of the sisters through that path. We spread our signature and footprint to mitigate risks. No hookups this time."

Yehudith approved the decision.

Amahle resumed, pointing at Rome, "Rome, we are going to drop down, you and I. Do you have my back?"

He looked at Yehudith and the other sisters, seeking their attention. "Always."

Amahle raised a hand and sought two neighboring trees by the edge of the sinkhole. She put her backpack down and retrieved a set of ropes. Rome obliged and retrieved his own.

Tick. Tick. Tick.

He asked, "Nine thousand feet. Do we have enough rope? We can't re-anchor further down."

"Yes. This material was designed by Yeh. It expands upon pressure."

His eyes widened. "Impressive."

The two tied complex knots around the tree trunks, anchor points for their descent. Amahle pointed at an overarching tree whose massive base hung over the sinkhole. "See this, Rome? This will be our second anchor point. We will drop fast, but we'll be away from the sides."

"Understood."

Amahle retreated to her sisters and Iwalewa. "Put your earpros on and go. I will see you down there."

The unit donned ear protections and performed one last gear

check. Rome followed Amahle to the crooked tree, a stack of ropes placed around his shoulder blades. They climbed the curving trunk and walked its wide base with ease, hanging over the bottomless sinkhole. Amahle tied another section of her rope around the base, with Rome finding another anchor point a few feet away.

She glanced at her sisters while hooking herself onto the second anchor; they had engaged the hole, following the natural trail. Yeh's reaper drone flew above them, watching for potential disruptors.

Without further notice, Amahle took a dive in.

Inhale... Exhale. Rome jumped.

They both gained speed and precipitated their fall, their frames rocketing past the sisters into the darkness.

Amahle's breathing control forced admiration. She addressed Rome through the comms as they reached the one thousand and five hundred feet mark. "Start braking."

Rome managed to issue an "Okay," his heart and lungs dropping as he plummeted. He placed his brake hand below his waistline and slowed the rope down, his rifle sweeping his sides.

Amahle had dived headfirst, braking with her right leg, her weapon aimed at invisible monsters below. Their flashlights attachments automatically turned on, dancing on the rich biodome they uncovered.

The two touched down and set foot on luminescent grass blades, dense and arranged in tight curls. There was no sun exposure in the depths of this access, yet the ecosphere thrived, enriched and diverse.

Tick. Tick. Tick.

Amahle and Rome swept the perimeter, both looking for hostiles. The place seemed empty of *immediate* threats, yet the abominations that were anxiety, separation, and dissociation subsisted in their minds. They both gathered at the center and unhooked.

"Cover me, Rome." Amahle retrieved a device from her backpack; it was a circular disc with a retractable arm whose end was tipped and sharp as steel. She planted the object into the soft soil and put her backpack on, looking at the faraway skies over and above, a speck in the vastness of this geological wonder. Her fingers found a rubber pad on her tactical vest and pressed it. "Yeh, do you copy?"

"Administrator. Loud and clear. We are halfway. Green status."

"Okay. I'm going to light the place up with a spotter. You know the drill."

"Roger that. I'll keep you posted."

Amahle motioned for Rome to get closer. "Rome, you've seen those before. Remember the protocol?"

"Yes. Go ahead, Ama." Rome began blinking rapidly, taking slow breaths.

She followed suit, waiting a few seconds before pressing her rubber pad twice.

The planted device illuminated the space with the brightness of a thousand stars, replicating the daylight cycle above: it had brought the sun to them.

Amahle peeked through an adjacent tunnel, where the Evil may lay. The passageway was curving left, its sides covered in fungi-like organisms. She fought an urge to engage the tunnel, called by a siren song whispering of treasures, and looked up; she could see her sisters five hundred feet above, rushing down. Iwalewa was carried through, her smaller frame easily spotted in the newfound artificial light.

Amahle pressed her rubber pad once more. "How are you, *Gogo*?"

"Tired, my child," she answered in a sharp whisper.

"I understand. We are almost there. Can you feel it?"

"Yes. There is something of value he—"

A seismic motion rocked the underground sinkhole.

Across from Yehudith's group, a shape emerged from the sides' grassy layers. It bore no face, as well as a body matching the scale of a commercial airliner; its three-fingered hands had no opposable thumbs. Grass expanded and retracted through its massive skin pores, and its skull was covered by a thatch of shrieking wooden birds.

The faceless monster broke free from the roots that had kept him caged.

Yehudith shouted, "Run, run!" Shots rang in the artificial light, as the giant sought its newfound prey.

CHAPTER 15
"TIME AVE. AND DREAMWALKER ST."

The wooden birds, they were admonitory in their collective dynamics. Their eyeless master was probing into her soul.

Yehudith ran back up the path, firing at the giant crawler swiftly advancing towards her. The sisters and Iwalewa rushed down, now a mere twenty feet from reaching Amahle and Rome's defensive position.

Yeh's reaper drone flew higher, monitoring the beast of no name's progression.

"Yeh! Hold it!" Amahle yelled. Rome covered the sisters as they arrived at ground level.

"Someone, with *Gogo*. The tunnel!" One of the sisters had already engaged the passage with Iwalewa in her arms. She dropped her and guided her to the left wall.

Shell casings rained from above in hot precipitations, their descent hushed by the thick, thriving sward. Smoke rose from the upper layer of soil.

The monster inched closer to Yeh, flexing muscle groups the size of wings; it was ready to pounce, leaning forward, indifferent to the high caliber bullets bouncing off its rubbery flesh.

Yehudith stopped and reloaded. The real-life nightmare charged.

"Zoya, drop a sonic charge! Five seconds." The reaper drone's nose dove in as it sent an ear-shattering shockwave through the sinkhole. On the steep sides, the bedrock eroded, carved out by the countermeasure.

The faceless giant retreated, its massive fingers digging into the rock as if it were dirt. Amahle, Rome, and the ground sisters ceased fire.

Yehudith ran down the path full speed, her Amazonian frame closing in on her unit. The wooden birds perched on the monster's skull swayed left and right in a vision of terror.

Amahle shouted, "AP rounds won't do it!"

Yehudith replied, while reuniting with her leader, "Botswana?"

Amahle nodded in agreement. The sisters grabbed fragmentation grenades secured to their tactical vests before the ear-splitting high pitch produced by the drone faded. The reaper returned to Yeh, flanking her side, awaiting further instructions.

The wooden birds turned towards the group on the ground, like zombified shells inhabited by a transient soul. The beast's skull and body followed suit, rushing the targets.

Rome engaged the tunnel, a smoke grenade in his hand.

Amahle yelled, "Now!"

The Hive soldiers twisted and pulled the frags' pins, then let the spoons go. They waited a couple of seconds, the faceless predator dangerously close, before launching the explosives; their footprints rushed to the adjacent tunnel, their shadows chased out by a massive detonation.

Rocks fell from above. A hacking sound sought fears to feast on; Amahle and the sisters raised their weapon, covering the sinkhole's access obstructed by dense smoke.

Silence settled.

Tick. Tick. Tick.

The smoke dissipated.

Tick. Tick. Tick.

The hacking sound morphed into a reverse snare as the massive golem fell to its death, its crooked flesh rocking the group off balance.

The survivors struggled to expel dust from their airways, dry coughs echoing in the gallery.

The fine dirt settled, and lungs cleared out in a painful process; the beast of prey was no longer moving. Its wooden birds had darkened, partially consumed by a searing fire.

A sister stepped forward to confirm the kill.

"No!" Amahle shouted. The sister halted her course. "Don't. This clicking, hacking sound. It was reversed at some point."

The sister finished the thought, "There could be one last countermeasure: Time."

Amahle nodded in agreement, picturing another sister dying to a threat beyond labels.

Beyond labels. "Where's Rome?" she asked.

Rome shouted from further down the tunnel, "Covering your exit! You're gonna want to see this, Ama."

The Hive and Iwalewa hurried to catch up with Rome, who threw two smoke grenades at forty-five-degree angles, allowing for a frontal field of vision, while exercising concealment from the sides and other accesses to this incredible underworld.

The underground cave before them was a residential subdivision the size of a city block. Carefully curated brick homes and manicured lawns were laid out in a flawless grid.

Mr. Powell was waiting on the doorstep of the central house, draped in an expensive-looking mauve suit. His warm smile stuck as he clapped.

"Congratulations on your new home! You may want to go inside."

Amahle ignored his recommendation and peered over his broad shoulders, through the closed entryway. She inquired, "Sisters, stay alert. Powell, what is this? What do you know?"

Mr. Powell stopped clapping but maintained his smile. He replied, "This is where timelines rise and fall. Where empires collapse. Where answers lay. Where neighbors may not be the most welcoming. One of them is... the 'Dreamwalker'. Get inside if you want to live."

Amahle raised her right fist and struck the top of her head once. The others stacked on her in a file. "Let's clear this home."

Mr. Powell opened the door and entered without reserve. Inside, he found a plush chesterfield sofa set up in the middle of a spacious yet homey living room space. Amahle and Rome rushed an adjacent room and swept it; they continued clearing short rooms at ground level while the sisters checked the upstairs in pairs.

Meanwhile, Iwalewa sat across Powell, cautious in her stance.

"Clear!"

"Clear!"

Amahle returned to the living room, reading into Mr. Powell's devious smile.

She finally spoke. "Clear!"

The sisters gathered downstairs.

Amahle asked Powell, "What's next?"

He laughed.

"Although I'm sure you'd be thrilled with exploring this area and losing yourself in it, I may have a few pointers that could provide you with the basic outline of a... roadmap? Ha."

He paused.

"Think of this place as a catalyst. Future timelines come here to seek answers but instead die, fed to the dogs and their master, the ones who constantly reshape said future. Past timelines... Well, I believe you are the only one that made it. So, I'm not sure. But one thing I can guarantee is... that an assault on the Dreamwalker alone won't resolve everything. You might want to explore the past a bit more, maybe revisit Rome's last days before he crashed on your shores?"

Amahle's eyes narrowed. "And leave my sisters exposed? With no guarantee of return?"

"I can guarantee your return."

Iwalewa raised her eyebrows. She smacked her teeth and asked Powell, "How?"

He approached Iwalewa and leaned forward. "*Gogo*, lay a hand on me."

Iwalewa touched Powell's forehead. She closed her eyes and remained silent, settling in.

Rome was studying the home while the eccentric god welcomed the wise woman's probing; there were no memorabilia, no pictures, no papers. The custom furnishing suggested someone had lived there, however.

The elder reopened her eyes. Her pupils were abnormally dilated, a coat of dust filling her wrinkles.

Amahle asked, "*Gogo*?"

"He's... he's telling the truth, for now."

Amahle weighed her options, assessing the risks in her saturated mind while inspecting the off-white walls this genderless home offered. This may be the last time with her tribe before she wandered in another foreign world, across an impenetrable veil.

As she contemplated alternatives, reality set in: This entire journey was a one-way forward-pacing trip, regardless. There was never a guarantee.

Finally, she spoke. "Sisters, we always knew this would be a delicate mission, oh? Something that is still beyond our comprehension. Rome and I may not return. Know that... I am immensely proud of your accomplishments and your contribution to our sisterhood, our eternal cause. You are the embodiment of excellence and unwavering loyalty. I love you all. And that goes for you too, *Gogo*. Yeh?"

"Yes, Administrator?" Yehudith was on the verge of tearing up, but her eyes expressed anger rather than sadness.

"They are in good hands with you. You are a competent warrior. Set a roof watch and stay sharp. Powell?"

"Yes?"

"How long will pass before we return?"

"With your time system, ninety-six hundred wave periods. Give or take."

She nodded, taking in this information. "Okay. Rome? Follow me. Powell, you're saying one of those houses out here?"

"Yes, Amahle. Rome will feel a particular connection with it. Open the door and enter the timeline. I will pull you back, but I can't disclose the specifics. I was not given much to work with, quite frankly. But I'm a creature of instinct."

Amahle smacked her teeth and left the house with Rome, renouncing her throne.

Outside, the strange sight of a suburban utopia housed in an underground cave still managed to surprise the duo. Rome walked the flawlessly symmetrical road they stepped on and headed towards the neighboring homes.

Although the residential properties were positioned with precision, they all varied in their architectural print and layouts. Art deco façades with bright pastel colors—Cape Cods, Rowhouses, Colonial ranches, contemporary block homes...

"I understand the sacrifices you're committing to, Ama. But I'm glad I get to do this with you. Grateful, even," Rome said softly.

One structure drew his interest as the duo swept a smaller perpendicular street.

A two-story townhouse stood, modest, in a secluded corner. There were jars set on the windowsills: They contained sands of different colors and calibers.

Rome stopped in front of the house, considering the light brown façade. Old double-hung windows gave it a quiet charm; he felt peace, and love, and joyful moments indescribable unless lived and witnessed firsthand.

"The jars. Someone we love collects those."

Amahle remembered her dream; how this young lady, Imani, crumbled like *sand* in her fingers. She breathed, "Yes. Imani?"

Rome paused. His eyes welled up; his face contorted in pain. "Yes, our daughter."

Amahle failed to fight her own tears. There was a connection with this other world, this other life her alternate self had experienced. She was compelled to fix this broken family unit, to explore something she'd never received before: passionate, affectionate love. Iwalewa was the closest to it, but she had never truly let the elder *in*.

Walking ahead, Rome opened the door and entered. She followed.

CHAPTER 16
"THE OLD NEW YORK"

September 6
2025

ick. Tic. Ti. T.

In the historical brownstone, light was buried alive by the blackout curtains of a curved nook.

Rome ran point on the incursion, his rifle guarding his steps, his feet tracking a trail of blood parallel to a marbled countertop. Amahle covered his rear, looking for evil spirits that may have hidden, shrouded by the darkest corners.

Blood began pouring through the cracks of the hardwood floor, vanishing from the scene. Soon, the parquet was left spotless.

The two remained sharp, their measured steps bridging the gap between them and a carpeted stairwell. They accessed the second floor quietly, looking for a threat or a presence.

The house appeared staged, uninhabited. Basic furniture in shades of white and oak fulfilled expected functions: a dining table, a sofa, a stand... There were no personal effects, no signs of recent occupation, no mail, no stains.

Besides the blood.

"Clear!" Rome shouted.

Amahle whispered, "The blood..."

He frowned. "I don't know, Ama, this may be from another timeline. Something that happened here, at an earlier or later time?"

Amahle nodded.

Rome looked around and locked on the stairwell. "I need to go back to this nook."

"Okay." They walked back downstairs, sweeping for further dangers lurking in the shadows. The nook was a set of three curved seating cushions and three thick pillows set up around the three-pane window, concealed behind thick beige curtains.

Rome sat down and peered through the curtains from the left edge of the frame.

Outside, a new world greeted the traveler. There was a circular plaza, a stairwell leading to the underground, and a corner store flooded by fast-paced patrons of all shades and sizes.

There were cars and buses, dogs and bikes. For a fleeting instant, Rome drank in the sensory input, confident his gaze would go unnoticed in this dense urban area.

The underground. His eyes returned to the green stairwell, finding a sign plastered above.

"Prospect Park. 15th St," Rome repeated, softly.

Amahle looked cautiously around, anticipating another trick, another intrusion.

Rome felt a profound connection with this world. It was his, his space and time, from before he washed ashore in Amahle's kingdom, bearing a gunshot wound on his forehead.

He pressed on his skin, where the bullet had entered.

Who shot him? Who sent him out beyond the Void? And why?

"Some answers. All the answers. It's here, Ama." The two gauged each other, one evaluating the other's sincerity, the other evaluating one's commitment.

Amahle finally caved and answered, "Okay. What's the plan?"

Rome searched the dark kitchen. Memories returned to him: Amahle, their daughter, this city. Knowledge proved invasive, firing in his brain unwarranted.

"New York City. Brooklyn. Across the ocean, beyond *Òkùnkùn. Prospect Park.* This was our first home, Ama. We used to take Imani to the park across the square. It was her favorite place."

Rome sat, quiet. The implications were many. *What of my daughter?* he thought.

Amahle said, "Rome, if that is true, we need an objective. She may not survive the *Great Fracture.* And we can prevent it."

Rome reminisced on simpler times, where he would move through life accompanied by the two most beautiful souls he'd ever been graced with.

Finally, he nodded. "We need to find out what triggered this fracture and why I was sent to you. The fact that I only belonged to one timeline in the Void, my abilities... There may be a connection with this... Dreamwalker. When did the *Great Fracture* occur?"

Amahle rubbed her forehead. "This is complicated." She started pacing. "*Gogo* mentioned an extinction-level event, four-hundred and twenty-one million wave periods ag—"

"No, no, Ama. We use a different time system here. It's based on numbers and counts, not environmental processes. Can you walk from point A to point B, through one wave period?"

Amahle complied and started walking from the nook to the kitchen. Rome counted on his fingers.

One. Two. Three. Four. Five. Six. She stopped.

Rome asked, "That's a wave period? I never thought of it before."

"Yes." She nodded.

"Ok, that's six *seconds* for the record. We need to leave, less armed. A lower profile."

They instantly took their tactical gear off and stashed their rifles and backpacks in a hidden compartment under the nook's seats. They kept their handguns loaded, tucked into their black pants.

Amahle took Rome's spot and peeked through the window; the street was buzzing, a gloomy sky caging the sun behind dark clouds. At this very moment, she was only concerned with the fulfillment of her objectives and the undoing of the *Great Fracture.*

She felt no significance here, no lost nor broken bond.

Yet.

Rome patted his head. "There is something I left here."

He moved the sectional sofa facing the kitchen and found a loose board. A simple pressure popped it out of its frame. Rome retrieved a green stack of washed-up bills and a key.

"Money. Like in your world, but foreign." He stuffed it in his pocket and replaced the board, then pulled the sofa back.

"Okay, Rome. This is good. You're reconnecting. But keep in mind, we don't have identities, an extended knowledge of the place, and alternate versions of ourselves may be roaming the city. We're not here to settle, explore, or practice extended surveillance. This needs to happen fast."

"I agree, Ama. And I count on it. So, how do we find out?"

Amahle paced around the room. "There was something unique about you. No one had ever crashed upon our world before. No foreigners survived the journey. You can cheat death. You cheated Time once. This *Great Fracture* is connected to you somehow. That's... that's certain. We need to find out what happened to our other selves. I assume Powell sent us here before the event took place. He may be devious and unreliable, but he is practical."

Rome understood. "There's... This place. Computers."

They both stepped out into the street, a cool breeze breathing hope into the tired travelers. Rome led them right into the pedestrian crowd and picked up the pace, matching the purposeful stride characteristic to the locals.

Brownstones lined up along the sidewalk, shaded by a tree line erected above vehicles and a few vacant spots. The memories continued pouring into Rome's mind, painful yet necessary.

However, the scope of his recovery remained local.

Amahle followed him as he turned right at the next intersection; she was looking for potential threats and spotters in this madness made of flesh and metal. While Rome followed the whispers of his recovered memories, she was moving through a foreign crowd, evaluating escape routes and anticipating aggressions.

She was the first Namibian to travel through time. Here, there were many more pale faces like Rome's and still, darker tones like hers. But no one seemed to find it odd; this city was a blend of allies, accomplices and enemies coexisting in harmony, a much more complex dynamic than what she knew of back home.

After a few minutes, Rome entered a small café, holding the door for Amahle. The space was match-box sized but mostly unoccupied. A strong incense burner rendered the atmosphere heavier on the lungs.

Rome asked the attendant, "Hi, computer please?"

The bearded man answered, "Spot two. Pay when you're done."

Rome thanked him and found a table with a number sticker on it, as well as a computer. Amahle pulled an extra chair, drawing the attendant's disapproving look.

"Some things don't change. Maybe we're suffering the same amount of exposure in this world." Rome pressed the *enter* key and opened a browser. "We share a last name by the way. Haviour."

Rome smiled at Amahle's surprise. He struck a few keys, hit the *News* category and reviewed the results. "Here."

THE NEW YORK TIMES
Opinion
Be Haviour.
By David Newnan - 09/03/2025

There is something outrageous about individuals operating beyond labels. How? How do you exist through various competing ideologies? How do you suggest and drive change when you appear lukewarm, when you are ideology-fluid, making bizarre claims like "progressive is conservative!"?

For more than thirty years, partisanship has radicalized: something we like to call "The Great Political Polarization of America". Republicans have hardened their stance, and Democrats have become more reactionary. And in the middle stand the people disinterested in this power struggle occurring between actors that are too big to fail.

A few snake oil salesmen offered a third alternative prior, the promise of a "doer's" policymaking: the folded sleeves, the cultural sensibility, the hip factor, ideas articulated in academic terms, data, the ground coverage... But none have kept their elusive promises, too busy finding a new angle in which they would, again, prosper. American society has even the most resilient idealists in a chokehold. There's no more trust in the institutions that serve the ones YOU serve.

This was my initial impression of Rome and Amahle Haviour, one of the most powerful couples you've never heard of. And, I must admit, I was wrong.

Rome is a British-born senator for the State of New York and a TV producer. Amahle is a world-class fashion designer and philanthropist of south African descent, a product of New York whose iconic fashion line, Ubuhle, is now the most valuable luxury brand in the world. As I'm setting shop at their Tribeca penthouse, I'm expecting more of the same: a bland speech on meritocracy, nonsensical guru talk, the love for us little people... Once again, I was wrong.

Rome loaded a new page on the search engine. "Forgive me Ama, but we are on borrowed time. Tribeca sounds familiar."

He typed, *Where does Rome Haviour live?*

Results rained down on the flat monitor. The first result was a preview of the most viewed article on the subject.

Rome and Amahle Haviour recently purchased a property at the exclusive Woolworth Tower Residences, 2 Park Place. The Penthouse…

Rome jotted down a few notes on a sticky note left nearby and closed the browser. He stole a brief glance at Amahle, her intense eyes briefly sweeping the screen, and they both stood.

The desk clerk nodded at Rome and said, "Three."

Amahle asked, "How much for those hats?" She pointed at a couple of black Yankee hats set on a rotating stand behind the desk.

He glanced at them. "Twelve. Each."

Rome understood. "Make it two." He handed the disillusioned owner two twenty-dollar bills, pocketed his change, and left the café in pursuit of his past.

As the two walked down Prospect Park, concealed by matching dad hats, Amahle asked, "How do we get there? You want to stake them?"

"Taxis. Less exposure than the subway. And yes, for a bit. We have to find out what happened to them. To us."

Amahle did not fully understand what *Subway* or *Taxis* referred to, but she trusted Rome's newfound awareness in this buzzing hive her other self was the queen of.

Rome raised a hand as they reached a wider road, waving at a yellow-painted vehicle, its headlights menacing in the gloomy day. The car stopped at the curb. The driver's window rolled down, and a rugged voice found Amahle and Rome. "Get in."

Rome opened the back door and let Amahle in first, scanning the avenue for watchers. The door closed after him.

"Where to?"

"Woolworth Tower, 2 Park Place."

"Alright, my friend."

The cab took off, bullying its way into the hellish traffic.

Amahle and Rome were both looking out the window, stunned by the heightened perspectives of what they called *home* in this world. This place was power, a cultural juggernaut that swallowed the least creative souls. It was both reward and sanction, death given in living.

Amahle followed a plane's condensation trail stretching beyond the skyscrapers. She felt conflicted, torn between the promises made to her sisterhood and a man who introduced her to a life-changing concept: She could be loved in different ways.

The Hive reproduced but men were simply donors, and daughters were favored.

It was transactional. Not with him, not here.

"We're here. Twenty-five dollars."

Rome handed the driver a fifty-dollar bill and opened his door. Amahle followed suit.

They set foot on a wide sidewalk dominated by a neo-gothic structure.

"2 Park Place, Ama."

CHAPTER 17

"THOSE FRIENDS OF YOURS..."

"Let's cross the street. People like them, *umuntu onemali*... They will be chauffeured to the concierge. I suggest we split up," Amahle stated.

Rome tilted his head in agreement. "Understood, I will post there by the street cart. You'll get a better angle from this little park." He pointed at a small square plaza operating as a roundabout. "One more thing," Rome added before handing Amahle cash. "Food and water."

Amahle answered, "Thank you. I brought something too." She shook his hands and handed him a small earpiece. Rome accepted and set it in his right ear as he crossed the congested street.

The improvised surveillance began, with Rome and Amahle seeking their alternate selves in the flow of commuters and visitors.

"Ama, how do you feel about all of this? Knowing I was honest with you. Knowing this is real."

The internal comms remained quiet for a few seconds.

"It's complicated, Rome. I can't erase my history with the

sisterhood and what it means to me. And if you're genuine, would you want that for me? Plus, I was thrown into this foreign world not knowing exactly what to look for. Or when we'll return. If we ever do, oh! I'm still processing."

Rome replied, "I would never suggest that. Thank you for sharing."

A couple of hours went by, the sunlight persistent in its ongoing feud with obscuring clouds. Traffic was constant, acting as a deterrent to anyone who could potentially establish that two visitors from another timeline were seeking their alternate selves.

Intrusive thoughts meddled with Rome and Amahle's stake-out.

A drive on the Amalfi coast.

Powell... What's his endgame?

I missed this city.

Will the Great Fracture's undoing... How would that work?

How much time do we have?!

She's beautiful.

A new development shut the thoughts out.

"Rome, black vehicle."

"I see it." Rome threw his empty coffee cup in a nearby trash can. "We're looking for anything of value. A stalker. Guests?"

Amahle remained silent, but he knew she was working an angle. From what he had gathered in isolation, she was a decorated warrior with an extensive knowledge in spycraft and surveillance.

The black SUV parked in front of the tower's revolving doors was on idle, drawing very little attention in this buzzy neighborhood. The driver left the vehicle and walked around to the sidewalk. He opened the back door to let the passenger out;

she was graceful in her exit and light in her steps: the *other* Amahle.

"Rome, this is my other iteration."

This world's Rome helped himself and exited from the roadside, seeking his wife. The chauffeur received something from the couple and left in his vehicle.

A few seconds later, another vehicle pulled up: a flashier, two-toned model.

Its coach doors opened automatically. This city's Amahle and Rome seemed to know the spendthrift couple setting foot on the busy street. Their smiles were wide and eerie and their movements almost theatrical. There was volume and texture in their fashion: teal furs and red coats, glossy heels and designer shades. New York's Amahle and Rome hugged them as they all entered the building together.

"Did you feel that?" Amahle asked.

From the visitors' point of view, the surrounding skyline began warping into distorted perspectives. Suddenly, bystanders began showing interest in the two, smiling wide in an artificial display of a fabricated courtesy.

Amahle and Rome began moving around, closing the gap between one another, a hand on their concealed guns.

The skyline stabilized, and the smiles faded. In the briefness of a snap, city dwellers had returned to their usual behaviors.

"Those two are the key, Rome. The flashy ones. But something is wrong. Time. The monster. It's here."

"Okay, Ama we ne—"

A loud sonic boom fractured the skies. The concrete began rattling underfoot. The people came to a scratching halt, turning their attention towards the two visitors once more.

Rome began running towards Amahle. As he closed the gap, his feet felt heavier and heavier.

"Amahle, someth—"

They were both sucked into a vacuum, pulled back into the aperture of an invisible portal.

AMAHLE - Tribeca - 2 Hours and 20 Minutes earlier

The Hive leader landed a heavy foot on the concrete. She was a couple of blocks from the Woolworth tower, finding her balance under the shade of a tree line.

"Ama, how do you feel about all of this? Knowing I was honest with you. Knowing this is real."

She was going to answer before she realized: This conversation had already happened. Looking ahead towards the Woolworth tower, she noticed the black hat at the roundabout. And the other black frame across the luxury residence they were staking.

I was sent back in time. And replicated?

From her experience in *Òkùnkùn*, she quickly understood that any contact with her future selves could trigger another fracture. She regained her bearings and slowed her breathing down, fighting a crippling panic attack.

Something in her peripheral vision drew her attention as she attempted to cage her pains.

Prints on the ground. No one seemed to notice, but she saw them slowly heading towards a nearby intersection. Amahle followed the lead.

ROME - Prospect Park - 1 Hours and 20 Minutes earlier

Rome landed on a hard bench, losing equilibrium as he grabbed onto the stone's edges. The canopy overhead triggered strobing visions of Imani.

Dad, how many trees are there?

A lot, baby. Hundreds. Thousands. They're essential. Very important. And we owe them the very same respect we give humans.

Okay.

Rome broke into tears. This was Prospect Park, two miles away from his first home, his current stash house.

He felt something in his ear. *The piece.* Rome tapped in and asked, "Amahle, can you hear me?"

Another loud silence reigned over the channel.

He was drained, taxed, tired of being taken away from the people he loved, his tribe. Rome sat there for a few minutes, fighting more tears. Some parkgoers stopped to strike a conversation or inquire about his wellbeing, but he politely declined any interaction.

He needed a new plan. When was he? Was it an alternate timeline? Or a different hour?

The stash house.

Rome stood and followed the twisted pedestrian lane to his right.

AMAHLE - Tribeca - 1 Hour and 30 Minutes later

The black footprints sped up past a sharp left turn. Amahle picked up speed, navigating through a mad crowd of busy souls. The skies darkened and rendered the tall buildings less imposing, their structure's outlines fading.

A couple of blocks ahead, the ground prints stopped and faced a dreamy antique shop with a dark green façade. Then the prints faded into oblivion.

Amahle entered the store. A young man with round-shaped

glasses and an athletic frame stood behind a counter whose intricate carvings depicted horsemen and sand dunes.

"Good afternoon. How can I help?" he greeted in a delicate tone.

Amahle smiled, looking around; it was bigger than it appeared from the storefront windows, the floor surface extending longways like a wide corridor. She replied, "Good afternoon. I live a few blocks down, the Woolworth Residences. I was looking for a unique piece for an observatory deck."

"Absolutely. Beautiful accent, by the way. How do you enjoy the new fitness facility on the thirty-second floor? A great addition to offset the basement pool's closure."

"I love it. I am huge on fitness. Quite the views, too. And thank you."

The antiquarian said, "I concur. Thanks for sharing, I was just curious. Do you need a minute?"

"Yes, please. I like to browse."

"Understood. We have authentic items dated back from the first Industrial Revolution. I ask that you please refrain from touching them. Let me know if I can be of any assistance."

He offered a warm smile and tone that felt genuine, reassuring.

Amahle replied, "Thank you."

She walked down the store, past the counter. It was organized in four aisles lined up with various treasures she thought belonged to a museum.

Amahle stopped by a nineteenth century Wooton secretary desk and swept the place, looking for a clue as to its significance in her quest.

A small courtyard appeared in the frame of massive French doors in the back. Amahle walked towards the back access, switching aisles, looking at gold-framed photographs hung on the wall.

She stole a brief glance at the courtyard's layout and noticed a door with a keypad right across from the store; it was a steel door with a thirty-inch protrusion.

Quite out of place in this setting.

Amahle turned around and stared into a metallic globe sunk into a block base. The antiquarian left his counter and waved at her, radiant. He approached and stopped six feet away; the man lifted his cream cashmere turtleneck at the waistline to reveal a handgun.

"I know you, miss Haviour. But something's off." He motioned for her to freeze. She obliged. "The Woolworth Residences. The fitness facility is on the thirtieth floor, and the basement pool was reopened in the mid-twenty-tens. And that accent. So, who are you, under that hat?"

Amahle readied. The antiquarian drew his handgun and inched closer.

She asked, "I'm sorry?" Fear seemed to have taken over her sharp facial features, disrupting the symmetry and perfect angles.

"I locked the store. There's no way out. So, one more time... Who are you?"

The barrel of his handgun drew nearer to her face. She weaved to her right and racked the slide of the gun back, effectively ejecting a bullet out of the chamber and knocking it off his hand. The man swung, but she was faster and far more precise. Her fist struck his elbow and his throat, and quickly, he found himself pinned down against a wall, fighting for air.

Amahle held his throat and moved closer. "I might let you live, but it's conditional to you providing me information. Nod if you understand."

The henchman nodded. Amahle struck his plexus dead center; the man's airways opened as he let out a dry cough. Her hand was still around his throat, strong and assertive.

She resumed, "I need to know what's behind that door in your courtyard."

The man hesitated, his eyes dancing between her and the courtyard.

"SPEAK!"

He stuttered, "It... It belongs to someone. It's a sto... stor...age."

Amahle stared into the man's soul. "Open it." She drew her own gun out, driving the man to the back of the store and out through the French doors. He entered a combination on the keypad.

10017. She memorized it and waited for the door to unlock.

Ahead, a small room filled with miscellaneous items uncovered many treasures: weapons, blueprints, art collectibles, documents in file cabinets... Amahle pistol-whipped the antiquarian and dragged him to a vacant corner.

Outside, a storm was brewing, the clouds further blackening and the wind rising.

Amahle rushed through the storage unit, reviewing as many pieces of evidence as possible. There was a picture: the eerie couple with the two-toned vehicle, their... friends in this timeline.

In the back of the photograph, a signature read: *The Lawrys.*

But there were other pictures, some of Amahle and Rome, attached to blueprints of brownstones labeled as *Rent-Stabilized?*

The weapons. Their serial numbers had been filed. The bulk of the room's contents was a mix of expensive-looking paintings and clothing items. Amahle's brain suffered sensory overload trying to piece the puzzle together. She went through the coats and jackets hung onto the various racks and checked their pockets and labels. Most were branded *Hardmond and Pearson.*

Beyond the storage unit, high in the troubled skies, something broke the barrier of the sound.

Amahle was pulled into another vacuum and vanished once more.

ROME - Prospect Park - 1 Hour and 5 Minutes earlier

Rome was tussling with a short, bald-headed mafiosi whose wide neck and big bone structure dealt rumbling blows. The Prospect Park stash house he returned to after his alternate left for Tribeca was ransacked, turned upside down. The intruder was already here, looking for hidden compartments and storage spaces.

Fortunately, Rome was no longer the pacifist the aggressor seemed to know of. He was trained by Amahle, in a world where mankind was conditioned for survival, and returned to New York City bringing this baggage along.

Blood began pooling on the floor, along the kitchen's marbled countertop, forming a trail leading to the nook.

The blo—

Rome's left kidney took a hit before he was launched into the stone wall behind him. His bones shook from the impact.

The aggressor tried to reach Rome's eye sockets, his hands dangerously close, but a kick to the bald man's kneecap threw him off-balance. Rome rushed forward and sent a right hook to his temple. The man froze and collapsed.

A *thump* hit the hardwood floor: the mysterious intruder fought a brief twitch and turned quiet, his leather jacket creasing on the collar. Rome felt his lungs practically ripping out of his thoracic cage. His vision was obstructed by bloody tears and sweat. The world around swayed like leaves in the wind, a rapid succession of images triggering an anxiety attack. He sat on the floor, propped against the nook's bench, fighting the storm within.

Dad, how many trees are there?

His breathing evened out; his sweating quickly lost its momentum. Rome was now shivering, staring at the man across the room, the one whose body laid dormant.

I love you, baba.

He smiled and murmured, "I love you too, baby."

His heartrate descended to a healthier range, and his vision recovered. The world no longer rolled side to side. Rome had managed to overcome his fears and collect his thoughts.

The door.

He used the nook's bench to stand and limped to the entryway. Rome locked the door and peeked through the nook's windows, wiping his bloody eyes.

No backup.

He took a deep breath and searched the attacker's pockets, finding a small notepad with scribbles was tucked in one of his leather jacket's inside cuttings.

06:45AM–07:50AM, MON–THUR, ROME AND AMAHLE. MORNING RUN FROM ROCKEFELLER TO WATTS AND BACK. NO STOPS. 35 MIN. NO SECURITY DETAIL. IMANI IS TAKEN TO SCHOOL. DO NOT COMMISSION CHILDREN'S "REMOVAL".

07:50AM TO 09:00AM. SEDENTARY. THEY PREFER BREAKFAST AT HOME.

09:00AM TO 09:50AM. HYGIENE AND GROOMING.

10:00AM to 12:00PM. Touring. Security Detail.

Rome skimmed through the timetable and stopped at 07:00PM.

07:00PM to 09:00PM. Dinner or socials. No executive detail. Lower risk – assessment.

Rome inspected the man's jacket. It was quality craftsmanship, a thick leather with neat and sturdy stitching. The label read *Hardmond and Pearson*. The aggressor did not carry any form of identification.

A professional.

All at once, the building shook. The brick walls rattled, breathing dust into the air. Rome grabbed the man's collar, fighting an invisible pull. Time eventually won the battle, and Amahle's partner dissolved in a vacuum.

CHAPTER 18

"IT EVOLVES. IT STRETCHES. IT OUTPACES ITS VOYAGERS."

Rome and Amahle - Morningside Park - 4 Hours and 25 Minutes earlier

Amahle was catapulted into motion on a set of steep stairs flanked by rock formations and chestnut oak trees. Her legs caught onto the momentum and slowly, she regained control of her body.

Further down, a man was leaning on the left rail. He turned around and waved. Amahle's vision slowly cleared and made room for the features she had become accustomed to: Rome's.

She ran to him and embraced him in a tight hug. He pressed on his skin, finding no scars.

"I'm not wasting that opportunity, Rome." In this unfamiliar world, she felt relieved reuniting with her anchor, the man who demonstrated he would commit to the ultimate sacrifices for her.

At this very instant, Amahle became the woman she dreamed about, in this study, high in the sky.

Rome held her face and kissed her forehead, cautious. "Ama,

you know I'm yours, if you ever change your mind. But we may be running out of time. What did you learn?"

Amahle saw the moment slip away, outpaced by the ever-increasing weight of her duties. But Rome was right.

She answered, gathering the slightest details about her encounter in the antique store, "We were sent back to a near past, but... duplicated? I was still in this place you call Tribeca." She paused. "But I did not communicate with our other... alternates? I heard them on the radio, though. Then I saw the prints. The ones who guided us in *Òkùnkùn*."

An old lady passed by. Her smile was distorted, eerily artificial.

Amahle smiled back and resumed, "It... The prints took me to an antique store. The employee there, he was armed. I handled him and I found this storage unit in the back. There were schematics, blueprints, art, weapons... Pictures of us and this... flashy couple."

Rome asked, "The memories are coming back. The Lawrys? The ones our alternates met at the tower?"

"Yes. Also, something about 'rent-stabilized' units. Oh and... a lot of clothing items from... What was the name..."

Rome added, "Hardmond and Pearson?"

"Yes."

Rome nodded in agreement and took Amahle's hands. "Okay. I fought an intruder who was searching the house we came from, the one in Prospect Park. He had the same label on his jacket. *Hardmond and Pearson.* Let's move." They started rushing down the stairs to a busy street. Rome was possessed with purpose. "He also had a schedule of our alternates' routine."

Amahle looked before her and frowned. "A hitman? *Inkabi.*"

"Most likely. Him and the Lawrys must be connected. But why and how? And where. And... when." Rome flagged down a cab driver who drove by the park's iron gates. "There's more information on your end. And the man may not talk, if we're lucky enough to locate him. We have to try your store."

The yellow cab stopped. They entered, and Rome instructed, "2 Park Place, please. The Woolworth Tower. Extra tip if you make it quickly."

The driver turned around and looked at them before nodding.

Amahle asked as the taxi drove off, "This process, us being sent back in time, it creates duplicates, hm? My future self may get caught when entering the store later on."

"What do you mean? I'm not following." Rome's brows creased in confusion.

"Well, if we reach the store right now, the shady clerk will remember us, and it will complicate things for my future self, no?"

Rome smiled. "Possibly. Great point." He whispered, "Do you suggest we take a different approach?"

"Yes. I have the code already. 10017." The two remained quiet. Amahle was considering the best strategy. "We're not equipped for an assault through the rooftop. And too much traffic."

The cab was swerving through a mesmerizing avenue whose heightened perspectives suggested power. The sun had just risen to the East, flooding the cabin with warmth.

Rome added, "And the antiquarian, he knows me too I'd assume. But what if we find a way to enter unseen, and remain in the storage unit until time runs out?"

"That could work. We need a decoy." Amahle slid closer to Rome and whispered in his ear, "I have smoke. An ordnance."

Rome's eyes sought something on Amahle's unremarkable black outfit.

She resumed, "It's concealed. A prototype. We shut the street down for a second, and you escort him out while the authorities of this world make for an effective distraction."

Rome nodded in agreement. The taxi slowed down to the curb of a wide pavement.

"Here."

Rome handed the cabbie a one-hundred-dollar bill.

The man gaped at the money. "Thanks, my friend!"

They exited the vehicle, with Amahle already veering left to the next intersection.

Rome followed her, looking for potential replicas spying by the newspaper stand or this green roundabout he'd always been so fond of.

She crossed the road at the traffic light, her steps purposeful, matching most pedestrians' pace; another busy avenue laid ahead, with shops of various sizes, scales, and foot traffic to their left. Amahle slowed to a halt, moving to the display showcases of a coffee shop.

"The store next door."

Rome glanced at the green-painted shop. The faded letters on top of the boutique read *Chez Cargill's*. He nodded. "Peculiar. Fine."

Amahle looked around, seeking a pattern in the heavy flow of citygoers. The street they stood in had consistent traffic. "Alright, Rome. You'll wait until the smoke gets darker and denser and the authorities show up. This technology is supposed to be long-lasting according to Yeh. Once they show up, you knock on the door and pull him out. We drop him off further out and enter."

Rome looked around and confirmed. Amahle pulled a small disc from her trousers and shook it. She kissed Rome on the cheek and hugged him tightly, holding the device in her right hand.

As he felt heat climbing in his lower back, Amahle threw the disc in front of the coffee shop's entryway. It quickly expanded before a smoke cloud detonated in the busy avenue, incurring panic and disorderly movements.

Most people ran across the street, zigzagging through idled vehicles, chased by a nightmarish creature they could not outrun, *fear*. Amahle and Rome remained by the coffee shop, blending in with a smoke that turned murkier by the second. Screams and side conversations populated further out.

Two minutes later, sirens flooded the nearby intersection. Strobing red and blue lights attempted to penetrate the dense smoke, feeble in their brightness and contrast.

Rome approached the store, running his hands alongside the coffee shop's boundaries and a portion of stone wall. Amahle followed behind. As Rome's fingers found the next door's handle, he frantically knocked.

No response. He waited a bit and knocked again, performing dramatic gestures. A silhouette drew its athletic frame sharper.

Rome shouted, in a raspy voice of a strong accent that was foreign to Amahle, "The cops are here! There's something going on! You've gotta evacuate, pal!"

The door opened; Rome offered a hand through the frame. The antiquarian asked, "What's going on?"

"Some smoke coming out of the coffee shop next door. I was getting my coffee when we were told to evacuate. I'm former NYPD, retired. I figured I would check next door. They have a checkpoint on Park Place. Safer." Rome's voice and speech patterns were unrecognizable.

The armed antiquarian hesitated.

Finally, he caved. "One second." He went back inside and returned after a few moments.

Rome was now fully camouflaged with this dark, smothering smoke. "Okay, pal, let's roll. The whole street is already empty. Reminds me of the pandemic. I'll take you further down and check other doors. K?"

"OK!" the presumed henchman shouted.

Rome's voice grew quieter as he walked towards Park Place with the antiquarian. He quickly returned to Amahle, seeking her contours in the odorless smoke.

They found each other. "Let's go," he suggested. They both entered the antique shop and closed the door behind them, effectively killing an invasive fog. Inside, Amahle headed to the courtyard in the back.

She asked, "What was that voice?"

Rome laughed and answered, "Something I used to do to make Imani laugh. It came back to me. This city loves retired cops. Authorities."

The two soon reached the courtyard and crossed to the storage unit's vault-like door. Amahle keyed the code in and unlocked the thick steel pane. They both rushed inside and closed the vault.

"We will run out of oxygen in approximately a hundred and fifty wave periods. We need to conserve energy."

Rome quietly agreed, fighting a crawling fear clenching his jaw. They began searching.

Amahle returned to the blueprints and notes. She began reading aloud.

"Rent-stabilized? High potential development in Fort Greene. Brooklyn Navy Yard. Two-hundred-million-dollar loss reported last quarter. Schaeffer and Nazarian are about to walk out. John at city council could plead for high rises and a mixed-use space given the zoning laws. One hundred and fifty acres. Annual ROI about seventeen per cent."

Rome paused his search. He said, "I remember. The Lawrys, this couple we knew... They are specialized in urbanism and real-estate development. The deals they made looked clean to us. But maybe there's more? Rent-stabilized." He scratched his forehead. "That is when a living unit is kept at a rate below market. This would make margins lower, or maybe prevent them from acquiring the site? Who are Schaeffer and Nazarian? How do we fit into this?"

Rome resumed his search and found interest in boxes labeled *Personal*. As he reviewed their contents, his fingers sought the rugged leather of a small journal buried under family memorabilia. He opened it and began reading the first page.

"Why let go of this power and capital? We've accomplished the impossible. Twelve percent of Manhattan's holdings owned by us. Orgasmic. I think of it when he makes my skin bleed and licks my wounds as he enters me. There's no limit, no boundaries. Laws are meant to be bent, to regulate the filthy peasants who add value to our investments but will never understand how to command and lead."

Rome paused and turned the pages, frowning. The air grew heavier.

"They're new money. An exotic couple with a certain appeal and... contained. Promoting all this meaningful charity work where they go boots on the ground and become this bullshit iteration of people for the people. She's attractive, though."

He looked at Amahle before he continued reading.

"I wish I was her, maybe physically and spiritually. But it's my nature. I'm an apex. A Jezebel. A Medusa without the rapes and the abuse. I'm all-powerful and almighty. Sometimes, when he's on a trip, I touch myself surrounded by ten million in twenties while the maid watches. She likes that. I have to give the peasants a sample of what my life is. All beneath me, including him. That's why. That's why. They need to disappear."

Rome turned the pages to the final words.

"H. will take care of it. He has them mapped out, for a lack of better terms. Bye bye."

Amahle added, "She's referring to us? Something happened in that tower."

Rome remained silent. He nodded in agreement, fighting the resurgence of painful memories coming back at the speed of light. They continued searching the storage unit, shielded from the outside world.

Another journal contained a list of locations.

20TH AND 9TH. LB.
60TH AND PARK AVE. NM.
P17.
G BRIDGE. CP.
72ND STRAWBERRY.

Rome sought Amahle's attention and added, "I think they hu—"

The very fabric of reality stretched out, colors and shapes distorted, distressed, spilling over beyond their known or perceived boundaries.

Within a millisecond, Rome and Amahle were gone, making room for a droning silence.

CHAPTER 19
"SHAPED IN A MUDDY NIGHTMARE OF LUSH GREENS."

"Sunflower!"

"Protocol!"

Amahle and Rome rushed to an entryway from both ground and upper levels. Outside, heavy artillery and high-caliber shells rocked the walls, cracked in a web of paint chips.

Mr. Powell appeared in front of the door, blocking the way. Amahle and Rome trained their guns at him.

He raised both arms and laughed. "Anyways, glad to see you back. There's a… war ongoing. Monsters. Plural. Tread carefully." He disappeared in a blinking flash.

Amahle and Rome spread out to the door frame's sides. The former was holding a sports bag in her non-firing hand.

"Our alternates brought the rifles and jackets back somehow, or maybe Powell. And the backpacks, I see. But *this*." Amahle pointed at the door. "This is still war in its purest form. Something we can't teach you. Are you willing?"

She ran a hand over her delicate features and looked up to a higher power.

"I... I see things, by the way. Like new memories from our alternates, implanted into my brain."

Rome answered, "Yes. To both."

Amahle nodded and rearranged her earpiece while Rome retrieved his bulletproof vest and rifle. She asked, "Yeh, do you copy?"

The silence gave way to a few more cracks and tremors.

"Yeh, do you copy?" she repeated, more urgently this time.

Rome readied his weapon, covering the entryway.

"AMA!" A cracking voice thundered through the comms. "This is Yeh! We found it! The Dreamwalker!"

Amahle gripped her handgun tighter. "Okay. Send me your location."

"Done!"

She turned to Rome. "Pull it from my backpack. The GPS."

He hurried and pulled a small wristband from the front pocket, then closed it back up.

"Here."

Amahle attached the device to her wrist. It instantly booted. She holstered her handgun, slid into her bulletproof armor, and grabbed her rifle.

"Let's go," she ordered.

Rome approached the door and opened it.

Outside, the underground suburbia was drowning in smoke, with craters swallowing melted homes. The air smelled sour, felt heavier.

Oppressive.

Amahle motioned for Rome to stop and asked through the comms, "Yeh! Fifty wave periods! Did you use a *mumbasa*?"

"Yes, Administrator! We were overrun!"

"Confirmed, Yeh."

Amahle and Rome quickly opened each other's backpacks

and pulled two gas masks; their integrated filter made the air easier to breathe, the pressure on their airways more bearable.

Amahle nodded at Rome, who resumed his dash. All around, the ghost town felt even more foreign. Something massive was crawling on the furthest steep sides of the cavern. Tracer rounds were chasing the moving *thing*.

Amahle ordered, "Right!"

Rome took a sharp right to a street overtaken by a bronze mist. Ahead, gunshots grew louder.

"Yeh! Friendlies coming from your western front!"

Their footsteps swept through a blend of dirt and shell casings. Sparks burst apart, splintering the battlefield into small, sharp fragments. The two rushed towards the sisters and Iwalewa, blurry silhouettes burning in the fray of a biochemical barrage.

The unit had set up a perimeter around the central house, Powell's bastion. Mortar rounds were still fired at forty-five-degree angles, dilating outward.

To Amahle, Yehudith's engineering prowess was unparalleled. How did she transport so many weapon systems? Yeh was a world-class magician whose tricks were safeguarded like gold; she would never share her craft secrets, instead working with compartmentalized cells of scientists to limit exposure.

"Yeh! Report?" Amahle shouted over the mortar rounds and sporadic rifle shots.

"We killed another one of these monsters. Similar to the one we slayed in the sinkhole, but with screaming mouths swaying on its scalp. There are two more out there. We lost two sisters in the fight. I'm running black on everything, I'm sorry."

Amahle laid a hand on Yehudith's shoulder while Rome assisted the sisters with the mortar fires.

"You've fought well, sister. The Dreamwalker?"

"Something even more massive in both scale and scope, Administrator. It only showed its shadow, but I knew that was *it*. Powell also confirmed. It's not conventional in its motions. It... it moves through space and time, but in a very tight 'bubble'. Back and forth. Time inversion, but localized and highly specific."

Amahle looked around. Afar, on the rocky walls of the massive cave, two beasts were evading shots, sometimes merging into one single shape.

"Yeh, you did well in setting a defensive position." Amahle pointed at Iwalewa. "*Gogo* is still among us." She paused. "We need to hunt, now. We'll find a way to put the Dreamwalker down. Pack it up. We'll be moving in twenty wave periods."

Yehudith confirmed and returned to one of the mortars set up at each corner of the house's front façade. Amahle walked among her Hive while deterring shots still rang, embracing Iwalewa's comforting hug.

"*Gogo*." Amahle paused. She joined the suppressive fires with her rifle while communicating through the internal comms. "Sisters, I'm proud of your efforts."

Tracer rounds ignited the cave once more.

"Rome and I were taken to a different world, with tall structures and crowded streets. People of all shades coexisting. It was before the *Great Fracture*. Our alternate versions seemed to have been hurt or killed by friends who plotted. We don't have all the information, but this may be why Rome crashed upon our shores. He was the other Amahle's husband, as he claimed, and he may be the key to solve this madness. You know, the sun never sets without fresh news."

Mr. Powell appeared by the house's entrance, rifle barrels temporarily aimed at him.

Amahle continued, "And Powell did honor his commitment.

For now. We're going to hunt the monsters that inhabit this hell and find a way to heal our world. Death may be the outcome for us, but we've done something significant regardless. Stay sharp. *Asihambe*! Chop chop!"

The unit began packing and forming behind Amahle, alternating between guards to keep the sectors of fire covered.

Iwalewa closed in on Amahle and whispered in her ear, "Child, Mr. Powell must die."

CHAPTER 20
"IT SEES WITH A THOUSAND EYES."

"Administrator, it's set. Twenty wave periods." Yeh shouted, sweeping Powell's central house's bricks with the manufactured eyes of a killing machine.

Amahle nodded and scoped the undefined monstrosities skidding in and out of a small access overhead. "Sisters. Rome. This is the last hunt. *Asihambe!*"

Her muffled voice struck hearts through the radio comms. The sisters, along with Iwalewa and Rome, readied. Amahle gained a line of sight on one of the flesh masses and fired. She began rushing towards a nearby street, one narrower than the position her sisters had been protecting.

The unit followed.

Ti. Ti. Ti. Ti. Ti.

In Amahle's overburdened mind, memories of her past and present collided into a beautiful confusion. She was no longer certain Namibia was her kingdom, nor the sisterhood her only family, but she knew one thing: Time needed fixing.

Up above, one of the massive beasts borrowing light from the small aperture began its descent into the underground suburbia, seeking its aggressors.

"Set motion charges left and right. All you have."

The sisters broke formation and began planting black circular devices on the buildings flanking the small street; it ended with a cul-de-sac dominated by an old stone house perched on a hill.

Amahle came to a halt and turned around. She stood at the edge of the driveway leading to the property that held the highest ground. Pointing to her left and right flanks, she dispatched the sisters within the dead-end's perimeter. Rome remained with her, with Iwalewa posted behind them.

Mortars launched nearby. Two sixty-millimeter shells ignited the air, shattering the aperture from which the beasts appeared. The detonation sent a shockwave to the houses below.

Yeh, a scheduled firing. Clever.

Fire melted the rock, expanding into a small mushroom. A scream forged in nightmares echoed in the cave's chamber; it was a hacking sound fluctuating in pitch, one that instilled fear.

Amahle swallowed and checked her magazine, tuned into the newfound silence. She looked above, seeing the hole was now sealed.

Her free hand found Iwalewa's shoulder. She pressed *Gogo*'s shoulder strap's rubber pad and whispered in her exposed ear, "Can he be killed?"

Iwalewa's tinted lenses found Amahle.

She said, "Possibly. I sense many futures. In one of them, betrayal will also be our salvation. And he will die."

Amahle ran her hand across her face and bowed. She returned to Rome, dutifully scanning the booby-trapped street. It was quiet.

"Did anything come back to you?" she asked.

Another hacking click grew closer ahead. The sisters watched the street while Amahle scoped out the house at the end of the uphill driveway.

Rome followed her sectors of fire and answered, "No. But how? If we were injured or killed, how did this cause the *Great Fracture*? We were powerful, certainly, but no global figures. No mention of time travel or maybe something more... spiritual in their notes. Why us?"

Amahle sought the telling shadows of potential threats up ahead and above. The home was quiet, still as death.

She sighed, "I don't know. But I suspect that if we... survive this, we may be able to prevent it."

And maybe stay together.

Underfoot, the light concrete shook. A dreamy eye as wide as the street swept up the road leading to the dead-end; dark spots, bubbling protrusions throbbed on its surface. The remainder of the beast's mass towered over the three-storied family homes built in the small subdivision. Its distinctive hacking cry delivered an unequivocal message.

Weapons raised, defiant. The golem whose living knives were dancing on its smooth scalp was a vision of horror, a creation that was rushed, patched together by a psychotic master.

Suddenly, its eye darkened under the progression of black vessels, as though shrinking.

"What are w—"

The monster downsized to a more human scale, its flesh blistering under the Kafkaesque metamorphosis. And then came the others: carbon copies, figures duplicated on an invisible assembly line. *They* began advancing, menacing in their overwhelming numbers.

"Hold your fire!"

Yehudith spoke through the radio comms. "The mines were

designed for a single target. The grouping... it's going to be harder to manage. I suggest you conserve your bullets and call your kills. Administrator?"

"Go ahead."

Yehudith stepped back and loaded her rifle's grenade launcher with two projectiles. She looked through an elevation sight set on her barrel and braced for the encounter.

The dancing knives were in sync, each clone following one of four travel patterns. Some ran the roofs, and some walked the narrow street path, while others crawled the façades or waited behind.

The hacking sounds returned as the beasts of prey picked up the pace.

BOOM.

The first bounding mines fixed on the buildings launched their charges and detonated in midair, deconstructing the horrors' bodies in uneven pieces.

BOOM.

Another directional fragmentation sliced their flesh and shattered nearby windows.

BOOM. BOOM. BOOM.

The air was filled with an iron-like smell, countless bodies falling to the IEDs set by the sisters. Yeh glanced at Rome, whose rifle was aimed at the masses rushing towards them a few feet ahead.

More of the monster's clones had crossed the threshold. They began moving faster, their three-fingered hands pouncing the ground as they charged.

Amahle ordered in a commanding thunder, "Fire! *AmaThongo!*"

High-caliber rounds were let off by the muzzle flashes of lethal weapons.

The bullets released flames upon contact, setting the otherworldly creatures ablaze. Small clusters of dark powder flooded the suburban division. The Hive and Rome backed up while Yehudith's grenade launcher provided barrage fire, sending dozens of bodies to their inexorable deaths.

More of the expendables had survived the Hive's first response, dangerously reaching close range. The rifles increased their rate of fire, and the radio kill counts ceased.

Amahle shouted over the radio, "Up the hill!"

Iwalewa was already headed to the stone house, in a grueling effort to overcome the accessway's incline. Rome and the sisters had thus far maintained their rate of fire, walking backwards to the driveway.

A few remaining beasts reached the sisters' closest quarters. The dancing knives on the monsters' dysmorphic skulls met their counterparts as the Hive engaged them with long, serrated blades and smaller handguns.

The product of an eternal war, Amahle remained on the frontlines, lacerating and shooting the Dreamwalker's agents as she faced almost certain death.

To her sides, two of the sisters had collapsed, forcibly merged into the flesh of the monsters who had become their greatest fear. A suction noise added to the terror-inducing nature of a place that was designed to kill entire timelines—and hope.

Amahle retreated and rushed through the driveway, Yehudith and Rome by her sides. A handful of sisters were posted uphill, providing overwatch and cover fire.

The Administrator grabbed a fragmentation grenade, twisted, and pulled the pin. She let the spoon go and threw the explosive device over her shoulder.

Atmospheric ignition surprised the pursuers, killing many.

Ripples made of flames billowed away from the grenade's point of detonation.

Amahle soon reached the house's entryway, looking downhill. She realized smoke had flooded the small cul-de-sac.

The hacking sounds ceased. Rifles were silenced as the few survivors began contemplating a meaningful death, embracing their purpose in the chaos.

The house opened. Amahle shifted her weight to cover the access, expecting a jack-in-the-box-like threat.

Mr. Powell exited the stone house, his layered cedar brown suit impeccably tailored to his flawlessly proportioned frame. His darker complexion stood out in a healthy shine, his curls of a moisturized brilliance. He was dressed and groomed for a special occasion, a once-in-a-lifetime event.

Oblivious to the surrounding chaos, death and the crippling panic rounding the mortals' flesh, he moved past the soldiers in a casual stroll.

His voice sang words in delicate notes. "H... It's coming. The one who fractured time? You have its undivided attention now. You'll get your answers if you bring it down, and I'd rather not miss this fervent display of courage."

Iwalewa moved closer to Powell, attentive.

He resumed, in a deconstructed and cryptic rant, "They will bathe at least once a day, sometimes two or three times, so as not to offend the spirits. Form composed of the quality of foulness, was produced hunger, of whom anger was born. And the god put forth in darkness beings emaciated with hunger, of hideous aspects, and with long beards. You were in Eden, the garden of God. Every precious stone adorned you. Ruby, topaz, emerald, chrysolite, onyx, jasper, sapphire, turquoise, and beryl."

Winds rose and sharp cries escaped their cage in a chopped

sound that rocked bones like a cold front. *It* was inching closer, heard but not seen.

Powell resumed his cryptic speech, "Ah. There you are! This is the part where you fight for her, Rome, where you back your claims. You better give it your all. I... wish to be entertained."

Amahle interjected, "This is serious, Powell! Tread lightly. Many sisters died here!"

Mr. Powell turned around and looked at Iwalewa. A shine in his eyes conveyed fear. "Of course. I got carried away. Forgive me!"

Yehudith approached Rome, breaking their silent agreement. "Stay ahead and provide rapid fire, no matter what happens. I have a way to bypass its time inversion tricks."

Rome nodded in agreement, peering through the rubble of the former street.

Suddenly, *it* appeared. A torment of an unprecedented scale. *Tick. Boom. Tick. Boom.*

The biped's monstrous shell was made of fungi-like protrusions shaped like ears; flapping scales set in a tessellation of wavy patterns. Through the lenses of inquisitive, blinking optics found in those protrusions, the Dreamwalker saw with a thousand eyes.

The chopped cries returned, stronger and sharper. The tone was deeper, the pitch lower.

It flapped its ears and eyes faster, issuing a terrifying warning in the form of a strong downdraft.

Suddenly, it froze.

Rome fired the first rounds, tears welling up in his eyes. The moment felt significant to him, definitive. As the shells of the remaining rifles began their charted course, ripples formed around the Dreamwalker, waves crashing above the group. The bullets returned to their senders, sliding back into the magazines and chambers.

The sensory input was unsettling; it was like losing control yet reaching a safe outcome.

Amahle removed her oxygen mask and shouted, "We have to find a b—"

Yehudith, posted behind Rome, existed in the Dreamwalker's shadow, its many eyes studying her. The sheer scale of the creature was unfathomable, its ability to conquer the very fabric of reality terrifying.

But the Dreamwalker had stopped its advance, its skips through space or time. Its swarm of optics shifted to Rome as it let out cries of lamentations coming from within, like the trapped and tortured souls of competing personalities.

Yeh, off the internal comms, retrieved a small circular device from her tactical pouch and spoke to it.

"Find R01 and launch."

In the intensity of this defining moment, she evaded scrutiny, leveraging the all-around mayhem and now-melting shells that failed to reach their target.

The disc emitted a strong white glow on its outer rim and left her hand, seeking a... host. It fixed on Rome's back and produced a loud, high noise. Before he could locate the source of the disruption or shift his body, Rome was catapulted by the disc's smoking propellers, launched forward towards the monster that danced on the waves of Time. He had lost control of his trajectory. His body barreled and shot through the sisters' peripheral visions.

The strange scene led to a temporary ceasefire. Voices took turns as they reached out through the radio.

"Rome?"

"Rome, do you copy?"

"Rome!"

"Ro—"

Yehudith turned around and aimed at Amahle. The latter gunned her down before she could squeeze the trigger. The sisters were confused, watching Yehudith's body bounce off the ground. She was now laying on her side, coughing up blood as she attempted to pivot back towards the monster.

Rome's frame was swallowed by the Dreamwalker, his brain muted by the vision of terror.

CHAPTER 21
"JUDAS AND THE BLACK MESSIAH"

"*P*ossibly. *I sense many futures. In one of them, betrayal will also be our salvation. And he will die.*"

Powell.

Amahle's face trembled in anger, her eyes flicking between the Dreamwalker and her second-in-command. "Why, Yeh? SPEAK!"

Yehudith was smiling, her blood spattering the lighter concrete she laid against. "Powell... knows... better."

Her eyes stilled, frozen in an eternal moment.

Mr. Powell approached. "Amahle, I can expl—" Before he could finish, his lips froze, stunned. His eyes swung left and right, trying to borrow from his peripheral vision. Iwalewa had placed a hand on the back of his neck, conjuring a paralysis, a deadly spell even a mischievous god could not counteract.

"Find yourself, child. Take your sisters with you!" she shouted over a brewing storm.

Powell's suit chipped like old paint. His flesh melted like wax. He became more and more unrecognizable before eventually disintegrating into fine particles. A black smoke wafted up from his ashes.

Iwalewa stepped on the black powder, tremored by pain, and raised a hand. The smoke returned and entered her shell.

"Goodbye, child of the sun."

Amahle tried to word a protest, but it was too late. *Gogo's* body had also crumbled, slipping through the fabric of her suit.

The Administrator was lost. Amidst the chaos of an unpredictable war, three of the most significant individuals in her life had left her. She trained her rifle at the Dreamwalker; its ears began flapping again, the many eyes rolling uncontrollably.

A voice whispered to her broken mind, *Even the most beautiful flower withers in time.*

"Move, move, move! Containment protocol!" Amahle guided her small tribe to the house uphill and breached in once more. The sisters followed her to a short room nearby, then laid flat on their stomachs, fingers interlocked over their heads.

Outside, a detonation proceeded to shatter all the windows. Walls cracked, and beams shifted. Glass rained down on the survivors, bouncing off their kit bags and bulletproof vests.

Amahle, raging in tears, stormed out of the house and raised her weapon.

Downhill, Yehudith's body had vanished, and the Dreamwalker was gone.

"SHOW YOURS—"

The suburbia's streets began shifting, slowly spinning on an invisible rotating platform.

Skyscrapers, sirens, and swarms of pedestrians introduced a new vertigo-inducing element to a nearby road. Amahle recognized the architecture, the sounds...

New York.

Amahle and the sisterhood rushed down to the cul-de-sac, a central hub for the ever-shifting avenues.

The City vanished in a blink and left room for pink waves crashing on black sands.

A body washed ashore, tumbling down the residential area's war-torn grounds; the waves reverted their course and took Rome back with them.

The vision ceased, and a young black girl sharing a striking resemblance with Rome appeared from a nearby street, joyfully skipping.

"Azza said Oluwa na him comfort me! Our greatest of the great!"

The little girl's outline dwindled and faded.

As the visions of a million lives continued materializing, Amahle addressed her sisters, the last survivors of a timeless war. "There is no snake that forgets its home."

They all hugged as the mayhem around them intensified.

"Home is where the heart is," answered the sisters.

The world around kept shapeshifting, struggling to produce a cohesive narrative.

T t t tikc. Titic. Tiiii. T t t t, tick. Tiuc.

Soon, a bright light set the place ablaze, effectively killing the dizzying visions.

Quietness settled, and Amahle remembered her *Gogo*, someone who she always suspected was beyond human, yet also so loving and trustworthy.

She remembered her fallen sisters, highly disciplined crusaders who feared no evil.

She remembered Yehudith, the Judas, the misguided who let a malicious spirit tear down every bridge she had crossed or built.

She remembered Rome, the man who shattered harmful

stereotypes and preconceptions. The one who suggested love was selfless.

At this very moment, she denied this war another fight, realizing her appetite for expansion and dominance was fueled by lacking something the *Great Fracture* had taken from her: him.

The encircling light grew feebler. Around her, the four sisters had removed their masks, prepared to embrace the purifying fires of divine judgment.

The eyes readjusted. Amahle closed hers and began praying.

"Created in a swamp of reeds, before you came to Earth. Conflated with the sky go—"

Sorrow flooded her bursting heart. She was denied love, her grandmother and mother taken from her, her closest sister gunned down by the very same rifle she held onto.

The ground felt soft underfoot. Muffled voices reached for her, slowed down by a masking veil.

Ti ti ti ti. Tick. Tick. Tick.

All at once, time resumed its natural course. Amahle's eyes opened to a penthouse bathed in dim atmospheric lighting. Outside of giant picture windows, the night gave the busy neighboring skyline a voice. Amahle recognized the structures.

"Administrator!"

One of the sisters had broken ranks and stood by a massive wooden table with sleek modern lines. Two other individuals sat at the table, concealed in the darkness of the section. Amahle raised her rifle, but the sister motioned for her to lower her weapon.

"It's you... and him."

The faces drew sharper features for Amahle as she bridged the gap. It was her and Rome, faces buried in the wood next to smoking plates; they bore a single gunshot wound on their foreheads.

She checked her alternate's pulse and motioned *No*.

Across the table, Rome began convulsing, gasping for air, pinned to the hard surface.

"Let's lay him down. Someone check the scene, the others, we need to staunch this bleeding!"

The sisters executed with purpose and discipline. One of them retrieved gauze from her vest and applied pressure on Rome's forehead while Amahle made a small cut into his trachea's windpipe with her blade.

"I need a tube! Clean!" Her hand waited for a tube. She received a small transparent silicon tube and inserted it into the improvised incision. A bubbly fluid escaped from the tube as Rome's breathing stabilized.

Outside, a sonic boom breached the dark skies.

Amahle muttered, "No, no, no, no." She knew of the cue, the public service announcement produced by an immutable force: Time in the flesh.

"What is it?" a sister asked.

Amahle answered, "We're on borrowed time, Iso. Keep his head straight. Any bleeding?"

"None apparent."

"Okay." Amahle looked at Rome's rolling eyes. He was fighting for his life, still pinned down.

"Please, fight. Fight, Rome. Fight to live another day."

Another sonic boom perforated the sky vault, shaking the penthouse's thick glass panes.

A familiar voice rose from the main hallway one of the Hive sisters guarded.

"Mom? Mom? Jezebel said you were sleeping. Mom!"

Amahle recognized the soothing voice, the articulate speech, the joy of a child who had never been starved for love.

Imani.

She exclaimed, "Imani? Wait, baby."

The sisters looked at Amahle, curious. Before she could reach for her daughter, they were pulled into another vacuum, losing sight of the penthouse.

There, at the edge of the universe appeared a maze, a cold place whose high walls were suffocating in their stature. Amahle engaged its corridors, her sisters trailing behind her.

But there were too many intersections and downslopes, half circles and loops.

Inside Amahle's fractured mind coexisted competing agendas: the hopes of reaching the end of this journey, the seductive prospect of a return to normal life, or maybe reunification with Rome, her husband from another world.

She sped up, fighting muscle failure, billions of atoms imploding within the confines of her brain. Her legs extended their strides, but there was a countermovement somehow: Amahle was now running backwards.

She witnessed her sisters pushed forward, helpless.

In the blink of an eye, Amahle was gone, drifting away from the maze.

CHAPTER 22
"THE BIG BAD WOLF DISEASE."

November 11

2025

Naushon Island, Southeastern Massachusetts.

I n the pitch pine and scrub oak forests hid a predator that was not endemic to this system.

Beyond, the ocean was quiet, trapped in a crescent-shaped bay that amplified the blazing stars above. A house stood on a slight rise, in between the tree line and the waterfront, remote and unremarkable.

Amahle's tears washed off her grimy cheeks, cutting through the blood and the mud.

Her eyes swept over the dense woods whose trees looked like geckos and porcupines. The barrel of her rifle begged for a threat, steadily pushing forward to the beat of her steps.

The modest home was swallowed by the edge of the forest, anchored into the ground, as if rooted in an unescapable past. Flickering lights brought dancing shadows to the back windows.

Amahle swept the perimeter and leaned on the back wall,

blending in with the wood. Her curls added volume to one of the windows' boundaries.

"See. I, *them*, know the value you bring. Pink horses and action soldiers. You're Santa Claus! Elves bound to trash quantum physics! Oh, this is good." The high-pitched voice resembled a failed attempt at a cross-species hybridization: rats and humans.

Another individual laughed at the deconstructed speech. It seemed to make sense to them.

The rodent-like voice resumed, "So, tell me."

"Indeed, indeed, indeed, deed. As you know, time is relative. An infinite number of ripples on an edgeless pond in which the world swims. Depending on your... perspective or speed, you can reach some faster than others. The ripples may look slower to you. Or more frantic. But *this* isn't about the rate at which you travel. Or your frames of references. Time is a monster."

The last sentence struck a chord in Amahle's exhausted mind. The second voice was raspy and struggled, yet familiar.

"It's alive, *them*, and all we need to do is provoke *it*."

The one he called *them* clapped. "Pink horses and action figures! AHAHAHA!"

Amahle took advantage of the celebration to peer through the window. Two men in white lab coats stood around a metallic cube hung on a translucid cable.

One of them was Rome. Amahle's heart dropped. This iteration of the man she put her faith in brewed darkness, his soul entrapped into a debilitating pain, one that appeared to exist beyond any known threshold. There were no physical clues yet, but she could sense a growing evil within his shell; cracks in his voice that masked something sinister.

"Right, right, right." Rome began pacing the room, looking down on the ground. The other was jumping in place, cheering.

Amahle swept the space for further threats and readied to breach.

But before she circled back to the entrance, the dancing lights inside produced a new angle of Rome's face, one previously buried in the shadows. Amahle stopped in her tracks.

He was disfigured, emaciated, his grayed skin tightly wrapped around sharp cheekbones. And there, on his forehead, laid a hideous anomaly: a fungi-like protrusion shaped like an ear.

Amahle leaned back against the wall of the wooden home, trying to gather her thoughts in this race against time. She peeked again to confirm: Rome's protrusion was still there, distinctive in its mushroom-like texture and particular shape.

The Dreamwalker.

Amahle found herself at the intersection of countless dilemmas, firing rapid calculations and exploring probabilities.

End them.

Kill them, save him.

Sabotage his research?

She made a quick decision and circled around the small cabin in the woods. The entrance was equally unassuming. She checked for wires, heat points on the handle and frame, and braced for entry.

The door flew under her raging charge. She neutralized the one Rome called *them* and trained her rifle at the survivor who once crashed upon her shores.

"Shh. Look at me," she ordered.

Rome raised his hands and avoided eye contact.

"LOOK AT ME, ROME!"

He finally looked, stunned by the sight of his presumed-dead wife.

"No. No. No," he muttered.

Amahle burst into tears, maintaining her threatening stance.

The sky thundered in a loud, deep bass.

Amahle warned, "We have very little time left, so listen and process quickly. Your wife is dead. I'm not from this world, but you came to me to save it. You caused the single most destructive event mankind has ever experienced. A fracture in time and space that separated us all. I can put another bullet where this parasite, or whatever that is, grows. Or you can come with me and abandon your research. And maybe, spend our last breaths together. Seek forgiveness, closure. Maybe."

Rome asked, "Pink waves and action figures?"

Amahle clicked. Rome was referring to their first encounter. *But how?* "Yes."

"Okay."

She grabbed a fragmentation grenade from her tactical belt, twisted, and pulled the pin.

Click.

He accepted her free, shaking hand as they exited the premises, headed towards the crescent-shaped bay. Amahle threw the grenade inside the waterfront property and let the blast consume the structure.

The skies warped in monstrous deformities. They were gone once more.

CHAPTER 23
"THEY BELONG TO ALL WORLDS."

"Administrator!"

"Sisters! Oh!"

Amahle and the lab coat Rome had returned to the stone house on the hill, the theater of the Dreamwalker's final slaying. The sisters were there, running up the path to bridge the gap.

Deadly winds pursued them. Amahle shoved Rome inside and covered her sisters, looking for threats other than the pressing weather phenomenon. The temperatures were unbearable, heat waves rising from the ground, scorching the outer layers of her skin. She rushed inside and closed the door.

"When will this madness stop? Is it an endless torment? The ancestors spirits?" a sister asked, frantic.

Amahle found a room to accommodate everyone and sat down with Rome. The sisters noticed his protrusion. Amahle raised a hand. "He's already been through enough. Yes, he's the Dreamwalker. But I don't think he knew."

Rome asked, "The Dreamwalker?"

"You created this hellish place and became a giant with a thousand eyes, manipulating time and space. You fractured this world. And then your past *and* future self crashed on our shores."

One of the sisters added, "The gunshot wound?" She pointed at his forehead's protuberance.

Amahle nodded in agreement. "It's a time loop, I believe. We saved him. He broke the world. But he also came to our kingdom to repair what he broke, somehow. He helped kill his own demons by merging with them. We survived. I saved him. He returns here, right now."

The house shook under the storm of blasting winds outside, rocking its foundation.

Rome spoke. "I think you just broke the loop by bringing me here. Time consuming itself, unable to handle the paradox of its disruptor and guardian coexisting on the same plane. Time is *alive*. Which also means..."

Amahle came to the same realization. "We are going to disappear."

"Yes. It is angry. And famished."

Amahle motioned for everyone to approach. They all joined hands, finding serenity amidst the loud sounds and seismic patterns.

"We lived well. We'll die strong."

Rome added, "I'm sorry."

Amahle sought his weary eyes, weighing the pain in his distracted gaze.

And there, Time collapsed on its own, swallowing the *was, is, and will be.*

EPILOGUE: LOVE YOU. ALWAYS.

The body washed ashore, sinking into golden sands, denying a soft current. A scar had formed an irregularity on her forehead, a tissue of a lighter shade of brown competing with her darker complexion.

Amahle's eyes opened.

She was alive, a rogue speck in the grand scale of NYC's very own *Coney Island*, an anomaly among the astonished bystanders standing at the edge of the ocean.

There was pain in her deep, rich brown eyes, yet hope beamed through the liberating smile on her battered lips.

Amahle was an outliver who had journeyed through the columns of time and space.

Soon, a couple dragged her away from the currents, further up on the beach. Someone checked her sides, gently pressing on her ribs. *Rome, please.*

"Ma'am? Ma'am? Can you hear me?"

Her eyes struggled to keep open but she nodded, her face buried in the sand. She sensed bodies gathering around her pulsing flesh.

"Give her some space!"

The man she heard laid her on her back and elevated her head. He spoke through a small talkie.

"Control, this is Chen, outpost zero-zero-seven, I have a black female, mid-twenties, early thirties. She washed ashore, approximately fifty feet east of Pat Auletta. Conscious but unable to speak. No apparent bleeding. I need transport to South Brooklyn Health."

"Chen, we've got you. Ten minutes out. We'll reach out to PD."

Amahle let out tears, blinded by the scorching sun of a peak New York summertime. The memories of a distant world leaked out of her brain, replaced by the comforting presence of a man who gave her his all. And their daughter.

She managed to look at the first responder, blinked to wash away the tears, and asked, "No hospital yet. I... need... Rome."

Chen was holding her head, examining her pupils. They were dilated, shaped like a sunless star.

"Ma'am, what's your name?" he asked.

"Amahle. Haviour. I... need... Rome."

"Rome?"

"Yes. Husband."

A couple of NYPD officers approached Amahle's crash site, setting an invisible perimeter around her beaten body. Chen rose and shook their hands.

"Officers. She is a bit disoriented, but no major injuries. She was brought in by the current while I was on safety patrol. She said her name was Amahle Haviour."

One of the officers nodded and stepped back. He pressed a radio strapped to his shoulder pocket.

"Central, this is ID one-nine-nine-zero-zero-nine-zero-six, I need a run on missing persons. Black female, mid-twenties, early thirties. Name incoming." The officer paused and returned to Amahle. He asked, "Ma'am, we're here to help, okay? Could you spell out your name for me?"

Inside her reconstructed mind, Amahle suddenly felt impatient, anxious to find *him*.

"A-M-A-H-L-E. H-A-V-I-O-U-R."

"Thank you, Amahle." The officer stepped back once more and reached for his shoulder's radio.

"First name is Adam Mary Adam Henry Lincoln Edward. Last name is Henry Adam Victor Ida Ocean Union Robert."

A minute passed, as taxing as the burning sun. The radio beeped.

"One-nine-nine-zero-zero-nine-zero-six, we have a hit. Amahle Haviour, former lower Manhattan resident. Was reported missing five years ago, September six, twenty twenty-five. The husband, Rome Haviour, made the report."

"Thank you, Central. I think we may witness a happy conclusion today. Count your blessings. Over."

Amahle overheard the communication. She asked Chen, "Can you ask... my husband. No hospital. I need him."

Chen gave her a comforting smile and turned his attention to the lead officer who had just ended his communication and was returning. His colleague was busy controlling the cordoned perimeter, sieged by curious bystanders. More NYPD officers had arrived, joining in to contain the flow of beachgoers, bloggers, and reporters.

"Officer. Transport should be here in two mikes, but she requested her husband first."

The policeman studied Amahle's flittering eyes and returned to Chen. "Okay. Chen, right?"

"Yes."

"Officer Mitnick, sixtieth precinct. I'll make a call. Can you assess her overall state?"

Chen looked at Amahle once more. "Pupils are of normal size now. No convulsions, tremors, no apparent neurological damage. No external bleeding or signs of internal hemorrhaging. Breathing is stable now, no airways obstruction. She may be in a mild state of shock but surprisingly healthy. I think we can treat her here and she could benefit from seeing Mr. Haviour, if we can locate him."

"Thank you, Chen. Let me see what I can do. Keep an eye on her, would ya'?"

Amahle clung to the hope of seeing Rome again, of holding her daughter, Imani.

The part of the fractured world she once ruled was now foreign to her, no longer a memory nor a far cry.

Amahle felt like she had endured so much but could not tell *how* or *when*. Her last recollection was a paved street in *Dumbo* and a power outage. Around her, incoming paramedics began taking her vitals, asking questions she found mundane and uninteresting.

Amahle wanted her family unit, the one she proudly claimed: the daughter who brought joy, the husband who brought love. Deep down, she knew they had not moved on from her disappearance, for better or worse.

She was now lying down in an ambulance, covered by a thermal blanket. The air had grown colder, life beating to the rhythm of beeping machines. Amahle sought peace in the neutral-toned ceiling she was staring at.

Tick. Tick. Tick.

Time went by, the sun shooting rays on the metal overhead, embattled in a formidable war with occasional clouds. Amahle burst into tears again, grateful to have survived and fearful of ending up alone.

"Where is she, officer?"

The voice made her heart jump and her vitals spike. She tried to sit, but a gentle touch convinced her to lay back down. Amahle found his steely eyes, as well as the beautiful features even her disappearance could not tamper.

Rome was here, reaching for her hand, stunned by her reemergence and the timelessness of her beauty. "Ama?"

"Yes, Ro. Baby." She smiled.

"Imani. Your mom. Your dad. Rowan. They're coming! I... I... What happened?"

Rome imploded in tears, repressing a sharp cry. His hands were bewitched by violent tremors. They connected, as two lost souls reunited by converging paths. He kissed her, their tears combining in a beautifully dramatic mess.

Amahle portrayed strength. "I don't know, baby. God, maybe? But there's one thing I've been dying to share. I need to tell you."

"Yes?" His hands gently pressed on her face, protective of the emotional injuries she sustained.

"To the edge of time. Love you. Always."

ARC READERS Q&A

Q: The opening scene was one of the best I've read! I have a couple of questions. What inspired this scene? I also noticed the parallel with the ending, what was the meaning behind that?

A: Thank you! The opening scene, where we witness Rome's arrival and uncover his particular... condition, is a commitment to the vision I had when writing *The Sunflower Protocol*. My intention was to create an opening sequence that would draw you in, with dynamics and imagery conveyed by the environment, which plays a huge role in this novel.

From the pink waters to the coal-black sands (Rome crashing upon Namibia), and the wave periods spewing him out (him existing outside of conventional timelines), every element served a purpose, tapping into the limitless character of your subconscious. I also wanted to create tension and mystery, which are very important elements in storytelling, and particularly in thrillers.

Rome's strange fate raises questions: Who is he? Why did he

crash on this beach? Who is Amahle? How does he know her? What's that gunshot wound on his forehead? How is he cheating death?

I'm really happy you noticed the similarities between the opening and ending sequences, from the syntax to the narrative structure and tone. It was, as you probably knew already, intentional.

Spoiler alert (!).

This entire story is a time loop, and it becomes more evident as we enter the last three chapters.

In the epilogue, Amahle is sent back to New York City, under mysterious circumstances, in an alternate timeline where she went missing five years prior. This is her reward for standing against the personification of time itself (The Dreamwalker), and for dismantling the Void. That is why Amahle shares a similar fate with Rome.

Now, why wasn't she sent back to Namibia? Because this sisterhood of hers, the Hive, as well as her kingdom would have never existed without the *Great Fracture*, which she resolved.

Q: Time travel is so fascinating. Noticed how although it's usually viewed from a scientific lens, it presents itself in many forms, based on the author's sensibility? But you took a more organic approach. What made you go that route?

A: I'm also (obviously) a huge fan of time travel stories and theories, and it did not just start with this novel. I remember scribbling some nonsense about toying with time when I was six, and I've studied the subject for years (I do not claim to be a subject matter expert in the field, though; we'll leave that to

ACTUAL physicists). But yes, we've seen time presented as branching and replicating (think Blake Crouch or the multiverse trend in film for instance) or it being a linear thread you can exit at various points, like a highway (*Back to the Future* or *Terminator*, among others). I wanted to branch out from the more popular theories about time and take a few creative liberties.

As I was brainstorming this project, I thought, *How do I explore this subject from a fresh perspective?* and that's when I realized: Let's make Time (with a capital T, yes!) a living organism whose body reacts to different things happening **within** (mankind, the animal kingdom, life, faith, all things…).

Q: Is Gogo/Iwalewa God? And Mr. Powell the Devil?

A: Ha! Great question. Before I answer that, you have to first understand that God and Satan (more specifically the duality of it) are primarily the constructs of Abrahamic religions (there are also mentions of evil entities in Zoroastrianism and other movements, but this is more of a reflection of the lower nature of man rather than actual entities).

In the Zulu religion, which Amahle practices, and within the African worldview overall, there is no concept of a devil that is in constant battle with God. There are gods and goddesses, and the ancestors' spirits play a huge part in those traditional beliefs. *Gogo* (meaning grandmother in Zulu) is a higher being yes, a figure close to a higher power such as God. She is one of the first ancestors. Powell, however, is more of a personification of our fears and our shortcomings than the actual Devil as we know it.

A strange one too, with its quirks (because don't we always try to rationalize things? Including wrongful actions).

Q: This is your first full-blown romance. What was the thought process behind that decision?

A: It's funny you ask because romance has always been something I was interested in and enjoyed, despite starting my creative writing career with more serious works. I love romantic movies and romance novels as much as I love my thrillers, espionage, or sci-fi epics.

But I'm not a huge fan of the more popular romances pushed in the mainstream landscape. With all due respect, I find those tropey, gooey, and often lacking genuineness because they are focused on fitting a certain aesthetic rather than delivering an actual message.

To me, romance is pure, deep, layered, understated and imperfect. Amahle and Rome's dynamic was inspired by projects like *Loving* and *The Sun is Also a Star*, where love is the colliding of souls, beyond labels and specific frameworks. I wanted to share my vision with the world and connect with people who had the same sensibilities.

Q: From my understanding, *Them* was Rome's assistant when he caused the Great Fracture, but who is he? Or, who are they?

A: I love that you brought that up. *Them* was initially going to play a bigger part in Rome's downfall and transformation, but I was satisfied with the narrative structure as it was.

I love to leave certain things to interpretation/imagination, so I'm going to refrain myself from sharing certain details with you, but the name was tied to his *split*: a multiple personalities disorder he suffered from. Also, *Them* simply showed up at Rome's doorstep after the latter survived his own assassination. Is he another evil spirit, like Powell? An ecoterrorist? A genius mastermind with a complicated past? The possibilities are endless, and it is for you to decide.

Q: Is there a special woman in your life? Someone you modeled Amahle on?

A: There are many special women in my life! Mothers, aunties, soul sisters, friends, mentors... I'm very private with my relationship status, but I can tell you that Amahle is (partly) a blend of my past relationships, some of the best I've had...

Q: What does the title refer to?

A: The answer lays in what a Sunflower symbolizes... This is a reference to the conclusion of the war, and the true nature of Amahle and Rome's relationship.

Q: I noticed that Amahle and the Hive spoke different dialects/languages. Yoruba, Zulu, Nigerian Pidgin...

A: Absolutely. And it was intentional. Since *Amahle-1* has expanded beyond Namibia in her world, to the Western and Eastern African regions during what she calls the "reunification" wars, the society she oversaw became a more fluid blend of various local customs and dialects, which she began borrowing from herself. She also formed alliances with foreign tribes (Azza being a prime example).

AFTERWORD

Unarguably, this was the most exciting project I've ever worked on.

No, this is no sales pitch (I don't do those, anyway).

But *The Sunflower Protocol* was written during challenging times: depression, the burden of single fatherhood, a soul-crushing corporate career, financial distress... It was an effective outlet I could pour in, the last refuge for my healing soul.

And, well, the subject matter.

Time travel has always been an object of fascination for me, from the short stories in first grade to the fanfictions in my teen years. This is also a project that I believe showcases my newfound maturity as a writer.

America is a Zoo was the first leap forward (one I'm immensely proud of), and *The Sunflower Protocol* is the crossing of a threshold.

Please consider supporting your friendly neighborhood independent author and review my works (the most important thing in my career right now) on Amazon, Barnes & Noble, Google Books, Apple Books, The StoryGraph, BookBub, and other available retailers/critics aggregators.

Thank you! Looking forward to exploring the next world with you.

Andre Soares

WHERE TO FIND ME?

Website: https://www.thesoaresprotocol.com/

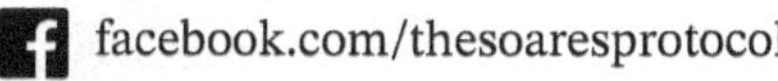

facebook.com/thesoaresprotocol
instagram.com/thesoaresprotocol

BY THE SAME AUTHOR

The Forerunner: A Vice Versa Series

C1: A Vice Versa Series

Alidala: A Vice Versa Series

America is a Zoo